PROPHETS & KINGS

PREQUEL COLLECTION

MESU ANDREWS

EDUTAINMENT INK

FOREWORD

I am excited to share with you the stories contained within this *Prophets and Kings: Prequel Collection*. Of course, the title itself uses descriptive words that indicate much about the contents of this work. The subject matter of *prophets and kings* points toward a time when Israel's human leaders were paired with Yahweh's representatives to provide protection and direction for God's people. A *prequel* is a story that precedes chronologically another story. A *collection* indicates that there is more than one of these stories presented.

So, there it is from my clinical, logical perspective. But those who have read Mesu's writing know that her stories are so much more than "head" knowledge resulting from strong research. Mesu's passion for the Bible coupled with her creative imagination yield heartfelt stories of human struggle and God's faithfulness. *Prophets and Kings: Prequel Collection* is no exception.

Mesu wrote the "Prophets and Kings" series of novels back in 2018-2020. Each of those works, *Isaiah's Daughter* (2018), *Of Fire and Lions* (2019), and *Isaiah's Legacy* (2020) followed the lives of both Biblical people and fictional characters. In the short stories of this collection, you'll learn some of the backgrounds of both heroes and villains. These prequels will help answer some questions you might have had about character motivations or their reactions that will now make sense in light of their histories.

As an author, Mesu delights in creating fun and interesting connections between readers and the characters in her stories. So, get out your copies of the full novels mentioned above and prepare to feast. But first, enjoy the appetizers of these novellas!

Dr. Roy A. Andrews (a.k.a. Author's Husband)

INTRODUCTION

I wrote these three books about prophets and kings because they're intrinsically tied together by the Crimson Cord of God's mercy. *Isaiah's Daughter* and *Isaiah's Legacy* both explore some of the most-beloved prophetic texts in Scripture. But how are Isaiah, Micah, and the other prophets mentioned during the reigns of Ahaz, Hezekiah, Manasseh, connected to Daniel and his ministry during the Babylonian exile?

The answer is found in God's Word, where Jeremiah clearly attributes the destruction of Jerusalem (and Judah's resulting exile to Babylon) to King Manasseh's sin.

> *[God said to Jeremiah,] "If [the people] ask you, 'Where shall we go?' tell them, 'This is what the Lord says: "Those destined for death, to death; those for the sword, to the sword; those for starvation, to starvation; those for captivity, to captivity." I will send four kinds of destroyers against them,' declares the Lord, '...I will make them abhorrent to all the kingdoms of the earth* **because of what**

**Manasseh son of Hezekiah king of
Judah did in Jerusalem.**'"*Jeremiah
15:2–4* (emphasis *added*)

Do you find yourself responding with the question: "Is God so vengeful that he would hold one man's sin against an entire nation for nearly two hundred years?" Many people have asked that question—which is part of the reason I wrote the *Prophets & Kings* series.

Sin began millennia before Manasseh's birth, but his heart was unfortunately the soiled waste pot that had accumulated the rotten fruit of his grandfather Ahaz's blatant idolatry and stubborn rejection of Israel's God. In *His Unfathomable Plan,* the prequel to *Isaiah's Daughter,* you'll meet the young prince Ahaz and discover possible reasons—based on biblical and historical evidence—that his heart might have been turned to idols from a very young age. You'll meet his young bride, Abijah, a starry-eyed priest's daughter who becomes the jaded queen that is Hezekiah's mother.

Two lovely heroines stand out in *His Unfathomable Plan.* First, we'll consider the fictional beginning of Aya's—Isaiah's wife— prophetic ministry and how she became a prophetess. Though her name isn't given in Scripture, her role as God's spokeswoman is attested. Second, we'll meet the prophet Micah's (fictional) little sister, Yaira, who becomes one of the key players in *Isaiah's Daughter,* and one of my favorite characters ever!

Adnah's Legacy will give you essential insight into the vilest villain I've EVER written. In *Isaiah's Legacy,* Shebna proves himself despicable—but in *Adnah's Legacy* we imagine him as a child. An innocent boy before the abuse and pain that maimed his heart and conscience.

Adnah was his first and only love—the mother of Meshullemeth, King Manasseh's eventual queen. *Isaiah's*

Legacy is a tough read because at some points it feels like the bad guys are winning. However, reading *Adnah's Legacy* helps remind us that even the bad guy was created in the image of the Creator—and we're all broken by sin. Both *Adnah's Legacy* and *Isaiah's Legacy* serve as a needful reminder that the only difference between the wicked and the righteous is our willingness to step into the Light.

After reading 2 Chronicles 33:12-13, we know that King Manasseh turned his heart toward Yahweh and away from idols —but the damage had already been done. His son and all but one king of Judah after him worshiped other gods and brought God's wrath to its tipping point.

Josiah was that one, faithful king who had four sons. After Josiah was killed during a strange battle with Egypt, Prince Nebuchadnezzar led the Babylonian army to a victory over the Assyrian Empire. Who was this Babylonian prince? How did he conquer Assyria—the centuries-old world power? Was he simply another cold-blooded, heartless, greedy emperor? I hope the prequel, *Of Heroes and Kings,* that imagines Nebuchadnezzar's courtship with his eventual wife, Amyitis, will help you appreciate the human side of the barbarous king we know from Scripture.

Nebuchadnezzar became Babylon's king when he was notified of his father's death while still at war in the Levant and western wing of his new empire. Daniel 1:1-3 says the young king invaded Judah, taking as spoils its handsomest and most brilliant young men. Daniel and his friends (Hananiah, Mishael, and Azariah—later renamed Shadrach, Meshach, and Abednego) were chosen as captives because they were either nobility or royalty. Were they King Josiah's grandsons or merely sons of noblemen? No one knows for sure, but the prequel, *Of Heroes and Kings,* explores one possibility that might help you understand both Scripture and *Of Fire and Lions* when you read the Book of Daniel in God's Word.

Ultimately, the reason I write any book, every blog post, or newsletter articles is to pique your appetite for God's Truth. My greatest hope is that the research I do and the fiction I write would help you read the Bible with more curiosity, understanding and excitement. I pray that you'll hear the God of All Creation speak to YOU the next time you read His Living Word.

In His Arms With You,

Mesu

HIS UNFATHOMABLE PLAN

Prequel to Isaiah's Daughter

PART I

UNWELCOMED CHANGES –
AYA'S STORY

ONE

*[The Lord said,] "When there is a prophet among you, I,
the Lord, reveal myself to them in visions, I speak to them in
dreams."*
Numbers 12:6

ca. 747 B.C. — Jerusalem — Aya

Aya gasped awake in the darkness, shutting out the haunting shrieks in her dream to hear the soft snores of her three little sisters. Shaking as if in the dead of winter, Aya rose from her sweat-soaked mat and looked out her window. The moon was bright in a cloudless summer sky. There would be plenty of time to tell Abba and Ima about the dream before the family woke. She had promised to tell her parents every time Yahweh spoke to her. The night visions were coming more often. This one had come three nights in a row.

Why have You chosen me, Yahweh? Please, choose another.

Her small room was littered with younger sisters. She stepped carefully over little Sarah and then over the two older girls by the doorway. Three more siblings lay in the main room.

Aya tip-toed over her brothers, past the smoldering cook fire, and stopped at their parents' bedchamber. Pressing her ear against the door, she heard the hum of faint whispers.

Why would her parents be awake? Cold dread snaked up her spine as a drop of sweat ran down. Surely, the dream couldn't yet have begun its fulfillment already.

She pecked lightly on the door and heard a halting, "Come in." The leather hinges groaned as she pushed her way inside. Abba's head lay in Ima's lap. Ima looked up, eyes pleading. "Another dream? Was it the same again?"

The answers stuck in Aya's throat when she saw her abba's red face, the bowl of water, and the presumably cool cloth Ima used to dab his fevered brow. Aya could only nod as her eyes filled with tears.

"Tell me again. All of it." Ima's tone brooked no argument, but Aya shook her head.

She refused to repeat the awful truths she'd spoken last night—and the night before. A plague was coming to Jerusalem. Many would die—including Ima, Abba, and Aya's three brothers.

Abba groaned and lifted his hand, calling Aya to his side.

Unable to deny him, she hurried to the straw-filled mattress, fell to her knees, and buried her face against his hand. "I'm sorry, Abba. I wish I could change the dreams or make them stop. I don't want to lose you and Ima. Or the boys. I don't want the death angel to visit Jerusalem."

"Go, to the Temple, Aya," he whispered. "Bring Zechariah here."

Her head shot up. "The high priest? Why?" Terror shoved aside her grief. "What will he do to me? I've heard people do terrible things to prophets who speak doom."

Abba's lips curved into a grin. "You know Zechariah and his wife Beriah would never harm you, my girl. They've been our friends for years. I must tell them how to care for my family when your ima and I are gone."

Aya covered a sob and frantically shook her head. "No, Abba. We must find a way to change Yahweh's mind. We must ask Master Zechariah to present an offering or—" Aya's panic rose with the ever-increasing resolve as she watched her parents' faces. "How can you be so calm?" she shouted at her ima, exasperated. They hadn't seen the vivid dream, the streets filled with mourners, every household in Jerusalem touched by death.

Ima kissed Abba's brow and gently moved his head from her lap to his lamb's wool pillow. She scooted off the mattress and cupped Aya's elbow, leading her away from the bed and keeping her voice low. "I remain calm for your abba's sake. I suspect I'm as frightened as you are."

For the first time, Aya noticed a sheen of sweat on Ima's brow, and felt the heat from her fevered hand. Ima swayed slightly, and Aya steadied her. "You are of marriageable age, Aya, but your abba has been slow to begin betrothal proceedings because Yahweh began speaking to you through these dreams. He asked Zechariah to inquire at the prophets' camp in Tekoa if a prophetess should marry or remain single."

Aya's thoughts swirled with the new—and unwelcome— information. "I don't want to marry! I must care for you and Abba and the boys and—"

Ima placed two fingers against Aya's lips, silencing her. "As I said, no betrothal proceedings have begun. Since the plague has likely started, your abba and I think it best if Zechariah and Beriah take you and your three sisters into their home."

Aya agreed for the first time. "Sarah and their daughter Abijah are good friends. But I don't need to be a burden to the high priest and his wife. I can work for someone else and earn an income to help with the three little girls' care."

Ima drew Aya into her arms. "My brave girl. I know you can

take on the world, but your abba and I think it best to have all four of our girls in Zechariah's care for a while. Then, at the proper time, your abba's position as second commander in the king's guard will leave a plentiful dowry for each of you to marry well."

Aya simply nodded and squeezed her ima tighter. Arguing wouldn't help. And she couldn't bring herself to tell Ima that in tonight's dream she saw the high priest mourning his own wife's death. How could Yahweh's high priest care for his two-year-old daughter by himself—let alone four more girls? Aya closed her eyes and inhaled the sweet scent of her ima. Lavender and honey.

Please, Yahweh, I'd rather be a poor farmer's wife than a prophetess of doom.

TWO

"Not one of all the Lord's good promises to Israel failed;
every one was fulfilled."
Joshua 21:45

Master Zechariah held his daughter Abijah in his arms, walking so quickly Aya found it difficult to keep up. She carried her two-year-old sister on her hip, while her other two sisters fairly jogged behind her.

They'd left Jerusalem immediately following the morning sacrifice on the first day the city gates had reopened. The mysterious plague, beginning with a stiff neck, fever, and headache, had spread through Judah's capital like a wildfire, killing hundreds.

King Uzziah had closed the city gates on the day not a single booth in the market opened for business. Mourners wailed in the streets. The dead burned in Ben Hinnom Valley. And Aya sat with her sisters alone for seven days in their house—unclean because they'd wrapped their family's dead bodies.

Her night visions had proven accurate to the last detail. But now a more recent dream cast a ray of hope into the dark corners of Aya's heart. Little Abijah looked over her abba's shoulder and grinned at Aya, waving timidly with a precocious grin. *Yes, that's the face I saw in my dream. Older. Radiant. With a crown on her head, she was seated beside a red-haired king of Judah.*

The joyous thought kept Aya's legs moving though they ached with the fatigue and sorrow of loss. She stepped around slow-moving travelers on the road south to Tekoa and called over her shoulder to her sisters. "Hurry, girls. Master Zechariah must deliver us to the prophets' camp and return to Jerusalem before the evening sacrifice."

Letting her gaze linger on the girls, she noted their stony expressions. They'd barely spoken since the high priest told them he couldn't care for them in Jerusalem. He said the prophet Amos had made arrangements for the high priest's daughter to live with a woman at his fig farm in Tekoa. And the girl to whom Yahweh spoke in dreams could live in a neighboring shack with her sisters. She must be with other prophets to hone her prophetic skills.

But a neighboring shack? Aya inhaled a sustaining breath and reminded herself that her parents had thought her old enough for betrothal. Surely, she would be capable of caring for her sisters alone in a shack.

"I know you girls are tired," the high priest called out. "But please hurry. I must get home before the evening sacrifice."

Little Abijah patted her abba's cheeks. "Abba go home?"

He pulled his daughter into a tight hug. "You're going to a new home, Abbi."

"Ima home?" Abijah's eyes grew wide, her voice full of excitement.

Aya's battered heart felt every bruise during the long hesitation. Finally, Master Zechariah answered. "Ima is in Paradise, Abbi. Remember? You're going home to Tekoa." The man sniffed back emotion, maintaining the control demanded of a high priest by the Law of Moses. He'd been unable to rend his garment or shave his beard in mourning as other husbands had done.

Perhaps that was why Master Zechariah seemed so unfeeling. Cold. And Aya had determined to be equally strong. There was no time for tears or weakness. Her sisters required constant attention. Aya had fixed their meals. Bathed them. Planned and packed for this journey. It had been two weeks since Aya had felt the reassuring arms of her parents' hugs. How long would it be until she felt anything but sorrow?

The sun was past midday when they crested the final hill overlooking the prophets' camp. "There it is." Master Zechariah pointed at a gated village in the valley below, an emerald jewel in the rocky-red Tekoan wilderness. "Amos and his wife, Yuval, are expecting us."

Flocks dotted the jagged rocks and cliffs surrounding the village. A thriving orchard bordered the east side of the valley, and fig trees in abundance sheltered stone houses from the harsh Tekoan sun.

The knot in Aya's stomach tightened with each step toward the city gate. When they finally reached the prophet Amos's doorway, Aya thought she might be sick. Before Master Zechariah could knock, a short, plump woman opened the door. Her smile drew them inside, and she patted little Abijah's cheek as Master Zechariah led them into the main room of the small home.

"Welcome, Zechariah," the woman said. "Please, rest by the table, and take your midday meal. I'm sure you're hungry." While the high priest settled himself and Abijah beside the table mat on the floor, the kind woman took Sarah from Aya's arms, her expression still warm but tears now gathering. "You poor dear. Did you carry this child all the way from Jerusalem?" She brushed Aya's cheek. "My name is Yuval, and you're a brave girl to care for your sisters through such a nightmare. Now, you must let the women in camp care for you. You're not alone anymore."

Mistress Yuval's kindness stripped away the armor that had shrouded Aya's heart since the plague began, and she dissolved into tears—then racking sobs. The woman passed Sarah to another sister and gathered Aya into a soft, warm hug. An ima's hug that felt like a soaking rain on desert soil.

A large hand rested on Aya's back, startling her. She looked up to a tall, thin man with gray hair. "I'm Amos," he said, warmly. "We're glad you've come to Tekoa, little prophetess." He patted her back and nodded toward the high priest. "Have you told Zechariah of the dream Yahweh gave you about his daughter Abijah?"

The sticky-hot air in the room suddenly cooled, and Aya felt Yahweh's presence as surely as Amos's touch. "I haven't told anyone. How did you know?" It was a silly question to ask Yahweh's prophet.

Amos simply grinned. "Yahweh told me you were the one to declare it to the girl's abba."

"What dream?" Zechariah rose from the mat and lifted Abijah into his arms.

Aya wiped the tears from her cheeks, now conscious that every eye in the room was on her. She offered her hand to little Abijah, who took it gladly as she'd done a thousand times before. "Master Zechariah," Aya began, swallowing audibly, "I saw Abbi with a jeweled crown on her head, seated on a throne, beside a red-haired king of Judah."

The high priest's expression was unchanged when he turned to Amos. "Surely, you can't agree. Royalty never marries the priesthood."

"Prince Ahaz has red hair." Amos lifted both brows, waiting for Master Zechariah's response.

"But Abbi won't be raised in Jerusalem. She'll be overlooked when the king seeks a nobleman's daughter for betrothal to his son. Why would he even consider the daughter of a priest?"

Amos ignored the protest and turned to Aya. "Because a prophetess will help raise her in this camp, and that prophetess will soon be betrothed to the king's cousin."

Aya nearly swallowed her tongue. He couldn't mean her. "You have another prophetess here?"

Amos' rich, deep laughter resonated through Aya, loosening her tension. "Perhaps I should have warned you before I declared your involvement in Yahweh's plan." He offered an exaggerated bow and peeked up from beneath bushy gray brows. "Would the Lady Aya be agreeable to a match with Isaiah ben Amoz, cousin to the king?"

THREE

"He who finds a wife finds what is good
and receives favor from the Lord."
Proverbs 18:22

A week had passed since Aya, her sisters, and Abijah had arrived in Tekoa. The five girls were given a small house to live in together, and Mistress Yuval's promise had proven true. Not once had Aya felt alone. At least a dozen women had checked in on them. They'd helped with cooking, took the two-year-olds for play time, and invited the older girls to find friends among other children in camp.

Aya stayed busy with daily chores: grinding grain, carrying water, spinning and weaving wool from Master Amos's flocks. Everyone on the farm helped with whatever tasks needed doing in order that the prophets could remain focused on their training.

The prophets. Aya wondered what it would be like to be a *real* prophet? She'd only experienced a few dreams before and during the plague, but the men in camp actually heard Yahweh speak. Since arriving in Tekoa, Aya hadn't had any dreams. Had they stopped because she'd complained about proclaiming doom? Or was Yahweh silent because in the secret places of her heart, He knew she was angry that He'd taken away her parents and brothers?

"I think you would spin a goat bald if it stood beside you." Yuval opened the door, chuckling. "I knocked, but you were focused on your spinning."

Aya looked at the basket beside her and realized she'd spun nearly all the wool while the other girls were out playing. "I'm sorry I didn't hear you. I've been keeping my hands busy so my mind doesn't work too hard."

Yuval tipped her chin up, inspecting her eyes. "I'd say your mind has been working even harder than your hands. Are you worried about meeting Isaiah?"

At the mention of her betrothed-to-be, Aya's stomach did a flip. She took a steadying breath before answering. "A little. Master Amos said *he* received direction from Yahweh for this betrothal, but I wonder if Isaiah heard the same." She tried to keep her voice light, but her concern weighed heavy.

Yuval pulled up a stool and sat opposite her, taking the spindle from Aya's hand and laying it aside. "Isaiah was born into the royal family, but his heart beats to the rhythm of the prophets. He wants nothing more than for Yahweh to rend the heavens and speak to him as He does to Jonah, Amos, and Hosea." She grinned, mischief in her eyes. "He's a little jealous of your dreams and is honored to marry a prophetess. Amos says he's more nervous about this meeting than you are."

The thought was so absurd, Aya felt her lips curve into a smile. "Royalty afraid to meet a soldier's daughter." She shook her head. "Yahweh has a way of turning our world upside down."

"He does indeed." Yuval sobered and reached for Aya's hands. "But I've watched you during these past days, my girl.

You have the strength of a soldier and the grace of royalty. Yahweh's wisdom is apparent in choosing you."

Feeling her cheeks warm, Aya ducked her head. "Thank you, Mistress Yuval." She hesitated, wishing for the hundredth time her ima was here to ask all the questions a girl needs to ask when facing marriage. "When exactly am I to meet the king's cousin?"

"He and Amos should be returning for the midday meal anytime now."

"Now?" Panic shot through Aya, making her voice squeak.

Yuval squeezed her hands. "Remember, Yahweh has given you to Isaiah. You are a treasure in God's sight and a precious gift to the young man you'll marry."

Trying to sort through her ragged emotions, Aya's tears came unbidden. "I don't feel like a treasure. I feel like Yahweh took away my parents and then left me. I haven't had a dream since I arrived. If Isaiah only wants to marry me because I'm a prophetess, perhaps he's making a mistake."

Yuval kissed Aya's forehead and drew close. "I don't know why Yahweh took away your parents, but His silence doesn't mean He's left you. To the contrary. Yahweh has entrusted you with great hardship at a very young age."

"Entrusted me?"

"Yes, little Aya. Yahweh gives the most difficult trials to those He trusts will seek out the deepest corners of His heart."

Before Aya could ask more, a knock on the door stole her breath. She shot a panicked look at Yuval and found her smiling. "I told Amos to bring Isaiah here first so he could see how neatly you keep your house."

She hurried to the door, leaving Aya to inspect all the little imperfections of her home. A dirty dish towel lay on the table. Abijah's leather hair tie sat beside her sleeping mat, reminding her she'd neglecting to braid the little one's hair. Aya heard the door scrape against the packed dirt floor and immediately studied her hands.

"Welcome!" Yuval's voice was overly cheerful, and Aya wanted to wilt into the corner. "Come and meet Aya before we go to our house for the meal. Aya, dear, Isaiah's here to greet you."

Since there was no back door for escape, Aya rose slowly from her stool and turned toward their midday visitors. Amos's brows were drawn up with anticipation. At the first glimpse of Isaiah, Aya's breath caught.

He was nearly as tall as Amos with dark hair and intense, black eyes softened by long lashes. He crossed the room in four strides, led by a radiant smile filled with straight, white teeth. When he reached Aya, he lifted her hand to his forehead—a sign of fealty as if she were royalty.

Her lips wouldn't move. Her tongue felt weighted, her head completely empty. What could she say to a cousin of Judah's king who knelt before her in a prophet's brown robe? And why was *his* hand shaking?

Finally, he looked up, still smiling, and stood slowly. "Thank you for agreeing to meet me today."

"I didn't agree. I just found out you were coming a few moments ago." The shock on his face told her how awful that sounded. "But I'm glad you came," she added when Amos and Yuval chuckled in the background.

"Well, that's a relief." Isaiah squeezed her hand, and it was only then she realized he was still holding it.

She didn't pull away. "I'm only a soldier's daughter, and I haven't had any dreams from Yahweh since arriving in Tekoa." Surely her confession would change the dreamy look on his face.

It did. A shadow of sadness darkened his features. He dropped her hand and cupped her cheeks. "My abba is a potter —who happens to be the uncle of the king of Judah. And

Yahweh has never spoken to me. I'd say if you agree to be my wife, I'm marrying above my station."

Something in those dark eyes danced, and Aya knew then that she could get lost in them—for the rest of her life. "If you marry me, you'll have an instant family. My sisters and Yahweh's chosen queen of Judah are mine to help raise."

"I've heard," he said, grinning. "I'm an only child. I've always wanted a big family."

She saw mischief but sincerity in his eyes. "All right then."

"All right?" Isaiah dropped his hands and stepped back. "You mean you'll marry me?"

Shy again, Aya felt her cheeks warm, and she peeked over his shoulder at Amos and Yuval. "I'm not sure what to do next, but yes." She returned her gaze to Isaiah. "After all I've lost, I can only hope you are Yahweh's gift to me. I dare not dwell on the past and lose a future beyond my ability to see."

PART II

UNPLANNED ENCOUNTER –
ABIJAH'S STORY

Four

"It is good to wait quietly for the salvation of the Lord."
Lamentations 3:26

Seven Years Later — Tekoa — Abijah

Nine-year-old Abijah wept silently in the corner of the only home she'd known, while Aya, her friend and guardian, finished packing the kitchen items for today's move to Jerusalem.

"If you're not going to help," Aya said, adjusting her newborn in the sling, "you should at least go say goodbye to our friends while Isaiah packs the cart."

"I already said goodbye." Abijah buried her face in her hands. "I don't want to see anyone. Let's just go." Aya's two-year-old son, Jashub, patted Abijah's back, but she groaned and turned toward the wall. She couldn't bear even her favorite little one this morning.

Abijah heard the door scrape over the packed dirt floor. "Go outside with your abba." Aya must have steered Jashub toward the door because then she shouted, "Isaiah, I have the last two baskets ready for the cart. Abijah and I will bring them out when we come."

More scraping, and the door clicked shut. A gentle hand landed on Abijah's shoulder, but she didn't look up. "I know it's hard to leave the prophet's camp," Aya began. "My friends are here, too, but Judah is changing, Abbi, and we must change with it. Prince Jotham was made co-regent when King Uzziah was stricken with leprosy. Now as *King* Jotham, he needs Isaiah's help to rule from Jerusalem." Aya tipped up her chin. "We go where Isaiah goes, my friend."

"But what about your sisters? They still need you."

Aya wiped fresh tears from Abijah's cheeks. "Sarah will soon be betrothed, and the other two are married. We'll visit, but you remember how the women of Tekoa helped me when Isaiah and I were newlyweds. They'll do the same for my sisters." She tucked a stray piece of hair behind Abbi's ear and searched her eyes. "But you, Abijah . . . You must live in Jerusalem so Yahweh can fulfill His plan for you. Isaiah told King Jotham about my dream—"

Abijah gasped and hid her face, heat creeping up her neck. She wasn't even sure she believed Aya's dream. It came ten years ago, and Yahweh had been silent since.

Aya tilted her chin up again. "King Jotham has asked to meet you, Abbi. He wants to meet you before you meet the prince."

A new wave of panic shot through Abijah. "What if I don't like Prince Ahaz? And what if—"

Aya pressed two fingers against her lips. "For ten years, you've pretended to be queen of Judah whenever you played with friends. You crafted crowns from vines and scepters from sticks. Trust Yahweh now, Abbi. His Word will come to pass."

Abijah dropped her head, resting her elbows on crossed legs. "A little girl's games are different than meeting a king face-to-face." Studying her work-callused hands, she voiced yet another fear. "What if Prince Ahaz thinks I'm ugly or awkward or timid and marries me only to fulfill the prophecy?"

Silence answered, drawing Abijah's attention to Aya's knowing grin. "You, my girl, are beautiful and graceful as a willow. Just the right mix of sugar and spice. Prince Ahaz will adore you." Abijah didn't dare ask the next question burning her tongue. *What if Ahaz is ugly, awkward, or timid, and I don't want to marry him?*

Before Abijah could produce a more appropriate question, Aya hurried toward the final two baskets in the house. "Come now, Abbi. Enough brooding. One basket for you to carry and one for me." She nudged the smaller one toward Abijah with her foot and hoisted the larger one into her arms, resting it on her hip. "We'll see if there's room on the cart for these. If not, we'll have to carry them."

"Carry them all the way to Jerusalem?" Abijah regretted her tone the moment her words escaped.

Aya raised a brow, suddenly guardian instead of friend. "I was more than patient when you refused to help me pack."

Abijah rushed to pick up the assigned basket. "I know. I'm sorry." Aya's expression softened as Abbi raced to appease. "I'll help more when we get to Jerusalem. I promise."

Aya gave a tight-lipped nod and headed toward the door.

But Abijah lingered in their Tekoan home, the need to remember cutting her to the heart. She'd witnessed both of Aya's births in this mud-brick house. They'd become a family here. Would Jerusalem change them?

"Come, Abbi!" Isaiah called from outside. He was a good man, gentle and kind. *Yahweh, will Prince Ahaz treat me like Isaiah treats Aya?*

The thought carried her all the way to Jerusalem as she watched Isaiah and Aya interact. Even as their muscles grew weary under the loads they carried—Aya with her basket and Isaiah pulling a laden cart—they laughed together and spoke of what Yahweh had in store for their future in Jerusalem. The half-day's journey sped by as thoughts raced round and round Abijah's mind.

For the next week, she and Aya stayed busy cleaning out cobwebs and arranging their scarce belongings in Isaiah's family home. It stood at the end of a long row of noblemen's houses in Jerusalem's Upper City. The Upper market was only steps away, but their household had little need to buy food since neighbors welcomed them with gifts of produce and sweet breads. Some folks seemed friendly enough. Others seemed only inquisitive about seeing inside a royal family's house.

As a member of the king's counsel, Isaiah received a monthly wage. Upon receipt of his first allotment, Aya fairly danced in the courtyard. "Isaiah! This is more gold than we saw in a year at the prophet's camp. What will we do with it all?"

Isaiah chuckled and gathered her into his arms. "We'll apportion it like we did in Tekoa. We'll spend some, save some, and give some to Yahweh."

Abijah tried not to roll her eyes. "Why does Yahweh need gold?"

The jovial mood died, and Isaiah released Aya, turning a searing gaze on Abijah. "Yahweh doesn't need our gold, but we need to give it—to remember it's His, not ours."

She wondered why Yahweh couldn't appreciate furniture, servants, and food they needed to fill their empty house but knew better than to ask. Maybe someday she and Aya would be able to decorate lavishly like other noblemen's households and purchase a few servants at the slave market. For now, she would be satisfied to help present a thank offering for their household and visit her abba Zechariah—the high priest—at Yahweh's Temple.

On the morning of their eighth day in Jerusalem, Isaiah was at the palace, the little ones slept, and Aya spun a fresh pile of wool. Abijah arranged a bouquet of tiger lilies, the mundane task giving her mind time to wander. *When will King Jotham call for me to seal the betrothal?* She didn't dare ask Aya, lest she seem too anxious.

As if hearing her thoughts, Isaiah appeared at their courtyard gate.

She saw concern on his features and met him in two strides. "Has King Jotham rejected me?" The words sounded silly when she said them aloud.

Aya set aside her spinning. "Of course, the king hasn't rejected you, Abbi." She marched toward Abijah like a protective she-bear and glared at her husband. "He can't reject her when he hasn't even seen her."

Isaiah looked as if his morning porridge was suddenly lodged in his throat. "Actually, King Jotham *has* seen her."

Abijah rehearsed every moment of her days in Jerusalem. "How can that be?"

Leading both women to the wooden bench in their courtyard, Isaiah knelt before them. "Jotham spends considerable time on the palace rooftop. He noticed our family when we went to the Upper market and watched Abijah as she interacted with our boys, the merchants, and the people around us."

A peculiar chill ran up Abijah's spine at the idea of being watched—and then came indignation. "And what might a king conclude while spying on a nine-year-old girl?"

A wry grin tipped one side of Isaiah's lips. "He has determined that he and your abba Zechariah will move forward with a betrothal agreement. However, he doesn't want you to meet Prince Ahaz yet."

The blood drained from Abijah's face. "Why can't I meet the prince before Abba finalizes the betrothal?"

"In King Jotham's words, 'Prince Ahaz has not yet reached a level of manhood that would make him appealing to a girl of Abijah's grace and maturity.'"

Confused, Abijah looked from Isaiah to Aya and back at

Isaiah again. "What does that mean? Ahaz is three years older than me. King Jotham thinks he's not mature enough for a nine-year-old girl?" Both Isaiah and Aya were trying not to laugh, but Abijah saw nothing funny about it. "How can I be too grown-up for a boy who will begin military training in less than a year?"

Perhaps it was the panic in her voice that sobered them. Perhaps the anger or frustration. Whatever the reason, Aya nudged Isaiah and braced Abbi's shoulders, all teasing gone. "The king's decision is a good one. At twelve years old, some boys aren't ready to think of girls and betrothals. Jotham wants your first meeting with Ahaz to be a good experience, one where the prince is ready to meet his bride-to-be, and you are ready to meet the man who will protect and care for you forever. Waiting is hard, but we can either be embittered by delays or trust that they are part of Yahweh's good plan for our future."

I didn't like waiting, but I certainly didn't want to meet a silly boy if he wasn't ready to meet me.

FIVE

*"In the Lord's hand the king's heart is a stream of water
that he channels toward all who please him."*
Proverbs 21:1

Three Years Later

Morning larks sang outside, while Aya's sons played in the courtyard. The family had finished their morning meal and started a new week after yesterday's quiet Sabbath. Abijah balanced a hand mill on her lap, grinding this year's wheat while the old servant, Ulla, mixed the first batch of flour and began kneading.

Isaiah and Aya had saved Ulla from the slave market three years ago by purchasing her son's gambling debts. The son had absconded to Egypt, leaving his ima responsible for his poor choices.

Abijah looked up from her hand mill and studied the woman. The Law of Moses required all Israelite slaves be released in their seventh year of service—though few masters obeyed. "Ulla, what will you do when Master Isaiah releases you at your year of Jubilee?"

Ulla slapped a small ball of dough, then turned it to knead the other direction. She worked hard but was painfully slow. "I'll never leave this household," she said, slapping the dough and turning it again. "They've been too good to me to leave them without a servant." Her eyes misted while she continued her work: lifting, folding, kneading, lifting, folding, kneading. Did she realize it was her debt that kept them from acquiring other servants?

"Good morning, ladies." Aya arrived, her voice edged with forced joy. "Four guests will join us for the midday meal: the queen and three noblewomen."

Abijah tamped down her annoyance and adopted Aya's positivity. "How may I help?" Truth be told, every noblewoman in Jerusalem dreaded the queen's company. She was impossible to please and the center of every nasty rumor in the city.

Aya mouthed a silent, *thank you,* and offered Abbi a small basket. "We need a few things from the market—three cucumbers, apples, and pistachios. Can you manage alone, while Ulla and I continue preparations here?"

Delighted, Abijah set aside her hand mill, stood, and patted the flour dust from her hands. She tried to sound as grown up as she felt. "You'd let me go to the market alone?"

Aya sighed through a wry grin. "You're twelve years old, and I suppose I must let you stretch your wings." Abbi rushed to hug her, but Aya held up her hand, halting her progress. "Two conditions. Visit only the merchant booths you know and hurry home. We have little time to prepare before the queen and her friends arrive."

Abijah grabbed the basket from Aya's hand and kissed her cheek. "I'll be back before you know I'm gone." She hurried out the door, not even taking time to change her coarse-spun robe or worn-out sandals.

The Upper market was barely a stone's throw from their courtyard gate, but today's visit was a benchmark. Abijah felt like a grown woman. Chin held high, she swung the basket on her arm and sauntered through the crowded street as if she were the queen herself.

She passed by Aya's favorite booth, choosing instead to peruse other booths and enjoy her new-found freedom. Brightly-colored fruit and vegetables beckoned her farther into the heart of the Upper City's finest vendors. Freshly slaughtered meat dangled along the way, suspended by twisted-hemp ropes. Wool, grain, pottery, and fine-woven baskets testified to the skill of Judah's artisans and other craftsmen from the world beyond Jerusalem's walls.

While inspecting a stall of apples, Abijah felt the unease of being watched. She shaded her eyes and scanned the palace rooftop, wondering for the hundredth time if the king was spying again. She saw no one.

As she returned her attention to the apples, she glimpsed a small contingent of soldiers approaching on her left. The apple merchant turned his attention in their direction, and Abijah had the uncomfortable feeling the young man with the four soldiers was staring at her. She dared a glance in his direction—a red-haired, stocky teen wearing the purple cape of royalty, a soldier's skirt, and a sword. He smiled when their eyes met. She immediately ducked her head, turned her back, and tried to concentrate on buying apples.

King Jotham had only one son. Only one prince could wear a purple cape—Ahaz. She certainly didn't want to be wearing coarse-spun wool and worn-out sandals for their first introduction. She placed six apples in her basket with trembling hands, paid the merchant--without haggling, to his delight—and turned toward home.

But the contingent of royal guards blocked her way.

The red-haired prince stepped close and held up a lovely

blue scarf beside her cheek. "I couldn't tell from a distance if this scarf matched your eyes, but I see now they sparkle like polished obsidian." He stepped back and swept his hand toward the booth of silk scarves. "But if a different scarf would be more to your liking, please come with me and choose another."

Abijah could barely breathe, let alone speak, and she had no idea what to do next.

He removed the basket from her arm and set it on the merchant's table. "After you choose a scarf, I'll take you to the palace orchard. The king's apples are sweeter than any in this market." He cupped her elbow and nudged her toward the booth of scarves.

His boldness loosed her tongue. "Wait! I've paid for these apples. I can't just leave them." She grabbed her basket and clutched it to her chest. "I must go home. We have guests coming at midday."

"I'll send a message to your master's house that Prince Ahaz has need of you."

To my master's house? Abijah looked down at her clothes and realized . . . *He thinks I'm a servant!*

When she looked up, he stepped closer again, lowered his voice. "Please, walk with me in the garden."

As if in a dream, Abijah allowed him to guide her a few steps, but the warmth of his hand on her elbow seeped through her robe and startled her awake. "Please, your majesty, I can't. I..."

Sadness shadowed his handsome features. "My abba is 'your majesty.' I am simply Ahaz to one as lovely as you." His breath on her cheeks smelled of fresh cloves. "Please, can we pretend for a few moments that I am a simple man? Would you do me that honor?"

His plea nearly broke her heart and cleared her head enough to ask a perplexing question. "Why did you come to the market to look for a scarf? Why not send a servant?"

He took a step back, and she was afraid she'd offended him. But he nodded as if saluting her. "Pretty *and* an inquisitive mind. My ima is ill, and I thought a pretty scarf might cheer her. If you won't choose a scarf for yourself, perhaps you'll help me choose one for the queen." He offered his hand.

Abijah stared at it for a long moment and then back into his vulnerable features—a slight drawing together of his brows revealed the sorrow in his eyes. Timidly, she placed her hand in his, and then saw the remains of flour dust embedded around her nails.

Reality slapped her, and Abijah realized how utterly ridiculous she looked—dressed as a servant, ogling a prince. Cheeks aflame, she ducked her head in a hurried bow. "Please excuse me, Prince Ahaz. I must return home."

She scurried away like a spooked fawn in the woods, hearing the prince's frustrated cry. "At least tell me your name!"

Without a backward glance, Abbi hurried home, breathless. Aya would have to return later for the cucumbers and pistachios.

Six

"Our midday guests have cancelled," Aya said when Abijah raced into the courtyard. "It seems the queen fell ill sometime during the night."

Abijah stood like a stone, contemplating whether to tell Aya about her exchange with the prince.

Of course, Aya could tell immediately something was amiss. Placing both hands on Abbi's cheeks, Aya stared into her eyes. "What happened? You're trembling. Did someone try to hurt you?" Without waiting for an answer, she turned toward the house. "Ulla, bring a cup of water for Abijah." Then back to Abbi. "Tell me what happened. You're pale as goat's milk."

"Prince Ahaz tried to give me a scarf."

Aya's silence was deafening.

Nervous tension forced words from Abijah's throat. "It was nothing, really."

Aya stepped back and clasped her hands. "If it was nothing, why is your voice shaking and your neck splotchy?"

Why must Aya know her so thoroughly? It was useless to lie to her best friend. "Fine. I saw a red-haired young man with royal guards across the aisles at the market. Our eyes met. I turned my back, and the next thing I knew, he was standing beside me. He introduced himself and offered me a lovely scarf."

Aya looked like she might eat the prince for lunch. "Where's the scarf?"

"I didn't take it."

"Good. A proper man would never approach a lone girl in the market." She looked in the basket and then scowled at Abijah. "A man who fills your ears with honey before he's baked the bread cannot be trusted."

Abijah's fists instinctively found her hips. "What does that even mean, Aya? The prince and I have been betrothed for three years. What's wrong with a single conversation?"

"He didn't know he was speaking to his betrothed! What if Ahaz flatters every pretty girl that way?"

Abijah felt her world shift. "But he seemed so sincere. He said his ima was ill, so he came to the market to choose a scarf for her. The queen is ill. Why couldn't everything else be true too?" She felt her throat tighten but continued anyway. "Is it so hard to believe that a prince could think me beautiful?" The threatening emotions turned to a flood of tears—adding humiliation atop humiliation.

Aya held her, whispering against her head covering. "What concerns me most, my sweet Abbi, is that you don't realize how beautiful you are. Any number of men could have approached you in that market. You're twelve years old, but you have the body and beauty of a young woman. I should never have sent you to the market alone. Forgive me, my girl."

Abijah nodded, gathering control to speak. "I'm glad you

sent me to the market, and I'm glad I saw Ahaz. At least I know he thinks I'm beautiful. And at least I like the prince Yahweh chose to be my husband." They both grinned, wiping tears.

The courtyard gate squeaked and Isaiah entered, his expression grim. He swiped both hands down his face, looking more weary when he met their questioning looks. "We've been summoned to the palace—all three of us." Abijah's heart turned over in her chest. Had Ahaz discovered who she was? But the pity in Isaiah's eyes told her whatever the reason for this invitation, it wasn't good news. He held Abbi's gaze. "Prince Ahaz wishes to cancel your betrothal contract."

Black spots clouded Abijah's vision, and she felt herself falling. Her next conscious thought was pondering a smudge of flour on Aya's nose.

Her friend knelt beside her, pressing a cool cloth against her forehead. "You fainted, dear."

Isaiah hovered over her shoulder, worry having replaced weariness. "Yahweh has a plan, Abijah. Remember, He said you will marry a red-haired prince and sit on Judah's throne beside him one day."

The reminder did little to comfort. "Did Prince Ahaz give a reason for breaking the betrothal contract?" Perhaps Ahaz discovered his betrothed dressed like a beggar. Or maybe a girl who runs from a prince can't sit beside a king. Could a faded robe or a girl's choice to run ruin God's plan?

"I didn't hear the prince's reason," Isaiah was saying. "I only know his mind was made up when he returned from the market this morning."

Aya brushed Abijah's cheek. "You're very pale, dear. Perhaps Isaiah and I should go to the king and tell him you're not well enough to appear—"

"No," Abijah said, standing on wobbly legs. "If Prince Ahaz is determined to break our betrothal contract, he'll look into my eyes to do it."

PART III

UNHOLY ALLIANCE –
AHAZ'S STORY

SEVEN

"I am the Lord your God, who brought you out of Egypt,
out of the land of slavery.
You shall have no other gods before me. '"
Exodus 20:1-2

Same Day — Ahaz

P rince Ahaz paced in a lavish chamber that centuries ago
housed one of King Solomon's wives. The last room on
the eastern hallway of the palace's second floor, it was
not-so-conveniently located beside Queen Dannah's chamber.

She visited too often, and today, she lounged on his couch, a
cool cloth draped across her forehead. "Why do you care about a
servant girl who ran away from you in the market? You can
summon any of a dozen maids to your chamber whenever you
wish." She flicked a hand at her fifteen-year-old son, shooing
away his concern, and then rearranged the cloth on her head.
"The real question is did you get the coriander for my headache?"

"Yes, Ima. The maid should have brought your tea by now."

Ahaz saw his chance to escape. "I'll go to the kitchen and hurry them along." He was out the door before she could protest his departure or recite a list of ways he'd failed her.

Queen Dannah was the only ima Ahaz had known. His birth ima died while giving him life, and King Jotham had married Dannah immediately following the mandatory thirty-day grief period. Dannah was as rigid as her name—*God is my judge*—except when it came to matters of the Law.

Having been raised in Lachish, a fortress city situated on the trade routes in southern Judah, she held a deep appreciation for many gods. When Ahaz was young, she'd told him bedtime stories of Egyptian gods and Canaanite gods—keeping their lessons secret from the righteous King Uzziah and Ahaz's abba, Jotham. She explained that Yahweh's true name was El and though He ranked highest among the gods, he was only one of the many. Dannah taught Prince Ahaz to respect all the gods of the nations around them.

Her lessons had served him well, especially last year in his first foreign battle. During peace negotiations with the Ammonites after Abba's army had beaten them soundly, Prince Ahaz stood with Isaiah, Judah's foreign minister, while the enemy king bowed before them. Ahaz offered his hand, and the Ammonite touched it to his forehead—a sign of fealty and submission.

"All praise to the mighty god Molech," Ahaz said, "who has given you wisdom and honor to fight bravely and protect your people with a treaty of peace."

Isaiah glared at him, hearing praise given to another god, but no one in Jerusalem complained when Ahaz's diplomacy secured the Ammonites' annual tribute of a hundred talents of silver, ten thousand cors of wheat, and ten thousand cors of barley. Ahaz smiled at the memory as he arrived at the palace kitchen. He seemed more popular with Judah's vassal kings than with Abba Jotham and Saba Uzziah. At least the Ammonites acknowledged his skill with a sword.

"Why is the queen still waiting on her coriander tea?" He shouted over the din and instilled an instant pall over the kitchen slaves. Blank stares answered. "I'm going to the Throne Hall to speak with the king, and by the time I return to my chamber, the queen had better be finishing a perfectly brewed cup of tea." He waited until the smattering of, *Yes, my lords,* ended and then stormed out of the kitchen on his way to Abba's courtroom.

Surely, Isaiah and his wife would be there by now to begin the divorce proceedings—from a child he'd never met. What had Abba been thinking? Legally binding Ahaz to a marriage when he was barely twelve years old to a little girl he'd never met or even seen. The high priest's daughter, no less! Ahaz was only fifteen, but he'd fought more battles than some old men and known more women than his abba.

He didn't need a princess—or a priest's daughter. He wanted that servant girl from the market.

Halting outside the grand cedar doors of Solomon's Throne Hall, Ahaz waved off the guards who reached for the door handles. He stepped toward the closed door, stilling his breathing to listen to the voices inside. Only one voice actually. He strained to hear more, but couldn't make out the words spoken. The voice sounded like Isaiah's, and his wife was no doubt with him.

Ahaz inhaled a deep breath and reached for one of the door handles. This discussion shouldn't take long. He'd return to his chamber before Ima had finished her tea. The heavy cedar door flung open, and Ahaz began his march down the center aisle toward three people standing before King Jotham's throne. His footsteps echoed in the near-empty courtroom.

Isaiah was first to turn, his recognition immediate, his bow compulsory. Next to him was a woman in her twenties, presumably his wife. Attractive, she averted her gaze and bowed to hide her all-too-obvious disapproval. The third was presumably the soon-to-be jilted priest's daughter. She remained facing the throne, stubbornly refusing to face him. No doubt, Ahaz's refusal would disappoint her, but she could stand in line with the rest of Judah. Ahaz always managed to disappoint those he sought to please.

"Son, I'm glad you've arrived," Abba said, a bit too brightly. "You're just in time to hear Abijah tell us about the encounter she had in the market this morning."

Ahaz nearly groaned aloud. Had she played with her prim little friends, pretending they married wealthy noblemen, who lived in fine houses and sired fat babies and provided servants to care for them? "I really must get back to Ima," he said, instead of voicing his thought. "She's still quite ill."

Abba issued that *Act Like a Prince of Judah* stare. "We'll both check on the queen after we've resolved your betrothal. Come, son. Stand beside me and talk with our friends."

Ahaz felt the familiar trembling begin, starting in his gut and radiating through him. He didn't quake outwardly. No. That would have been more bearable. This was an inner crawling, as if every muscle and sinew screamed to escape his skin. He'd rather face an army of thousands than these Yahweh-fearing people in whose eyes he would never be enough.

But he knew better than to defy his abba, the king. He straightened his shoulders, brushed by the girl who refused to acknowledge his presence, and ascended the six steps of the dais to stand at King Jotham's right shoulder. When he lifted his eyes, there she was—his servant girl in a fine linen robe.

"You!" he said, accusation warring with wonder. "It was you in the market this morning?"

Eight

"'For my thoughts are not your thoughts,
neither are your ways my ways,' declares the Lord."
Isaiah 55:8

The girl fell to her knees and then stretched out her arms on the floor. "Please, your majesty. I didn't know it was you at first, and then when you declared yourself, I was too ashamed of my appearance to confess."

The king gawked at his son, at the girl, and then back at Ahaz. "You mean Abijah is the servant girl you demanded we find?"

Abijah's head popped up. "You wanted to find me?"

Heat crept up Ahaz's neck and cheeks. He couldn't decide whether to be angry or ecstatic, but he was most certainly embarrassed. He would not have his heart laid bare in front of this girl and her guardians. "Out!" He shouted at Isaiah and then turned to his abba. "I want them out while I speak with you privately."

The king's eyes narrowed and he nodded silent assent. Isaiah gathered the two women under his arms and retreated from the room. Abba waited for the cedar doors to click shut before he stood and turned his simmering anger on Ahaz. "When will you learn to rein your emotions? Honestly!"

He inhaled a calming breath and released a sigh. But Ahaz knew his abba's lecture had only begun. "One encounter with a girl in the market," Jotham continued, "and you're ready to throw away a three-year betrothal—ordained by Yahweh, I might add. Then, when Yahweh orchestrates a meeting for you two in the market, your emotions toss you like the waves of the sea, and you shout at the young woman you were willing to search the ends of the earth to find." He placed his hand on Ahaz's shoulder and squeezed. "Wisdom comes in calm deliberation, my son. Please, *please* cultivate a measure of it soon."

What was Ahaz supposed to say now? Had Yahweh orchestrated the meeting in the market? Possibly. Dannah always said Yahweh chose favorites, and Ahaz wasn't one of them. It made sense that Yahweh would arrange for Ahaz to make a fool of himself with the only girl that had ever moved his heart. How could he explain to Abijah, to anyone—even to himself—how he'd felt when he saw her in the market this morning? More than her beauty drew him, though she was the most beautiful woman he'd ever seen. Sparkling black eyes that danced with emotion. Alabaster skin that glowed in the morning sun. And soft curves that spoke of womanhood even though she was only twelve. Regardless of Yahweh's tricks, Ahaz wanted this girl.

He donned his most penitent expression and bowed. "I'm sorry for the way I behaved, Abba. Let's bring Isaiah and his wife back in, and I will apologize. Then, I'd like to assure Abijah of my intent to marry her—immediately."

"Ahaz!" Jotham huffed. "Will you never heed my warning to control your emotions?"

Ahaz raised his head, a mischievous grin meeting his abba's frustration. "I suppose we could wait a month to marry if you think it wiser to do so." His charm and wit had saved Ahaz from many arguments, and he watched it dissolve the brittle edges around his abba's heart even now.

A slight grin broke through Jotham's stern expression. "I'm glad you like her."

"When I look at her, Abba, I feel like I've never felt before. I want to protect her. I want to know what she's thinking. What she likes and doesn't like. I want to—" Ahaz felt warmth creep up his neck again at the thought of their wedding night. He ducked his head. When had he become a pious, shy maiden?

Abba placed a hand on his shoulder. "Look at me, son." Ahaz obeyed, and the king raised a stern brow. "I will negotiate a wedding date that considers Abijah's well-being. It's not safe for a girl to conceive before her body is ready to give birth, and I'm sure you'll want a son soon after you marry."

When Ahaz opened his mouth to protest, the king lifted his hand, stifling any negotiations.

"All right, Abba, but soon. Tell Isaiah the wedding must be soon."

The king chuckled and resumed his seat on the throne, nodding to the guards at the rear doors to invite their guests to return. Isaiah entered first, followed by his wife, and Abijah trailed behind. Ahaz tried to see her face, but she kept her head bowed. Had his temper shaken her? He must make it up to her somehow.

Before Isaiah reached the edge of the crimson carpet, where petitioners stood before the king, Ahaz descended the dais and hurried to Abijah's side. Startled, she looked up with those polished-obsidian eyes and asked a million questions without saying a word.

Ahaz offered his left arm, and then lifted her hand to rest it on his forearm. "Let me escort you like the queen you will someday be."

Her lips parted with a little gasp—and then a glowing smile.

His reward. They followed Isaiah and his wife, all four stopping at the edge of the crimson carpet, waiting before Judah's king.

"Isaiah ben Amoz," King Jotham began, "my son will honor the betrothal contract, and we are anxious to proceed with wedding plans. Since you and Aya paid Abijah's bride price and have served as her guardians these many years, I will consult you rather than her abba Zechariah on the matter of a date for Ahaz and Abijah's wedding."

Isaiah exchanged a glance with Aya, who pulled Isaiah close to whisper in his ear. Ahaz tried to lean in to hear the couple's exchange, but too soon Isaiah pronounced their verdict. "My wife tells me that Abijah is physically capable of marriage and childbirth, but we would prefer the wedding be delayed until Abijah's thirteenth birthday—for safer childbearing."

Ahaz bit his tongue to keep from protesting. He'd pressed Abba today as far as he dared.

"We have one other concern," Isaiah said with a sidelong glance at the prince. "We haven't seen the king or Prince Ahaz at Temple sacrifices in quite some time. Since this wedding will be a national event, likely drawing guests from all over Judah as well as foreign dignitaries, we ask that the king and prince make a special offering at Yahweh's Temple on the day of the wedding."

"No!" Ahaz shouted. "We will not step foot in that place!"

"Ahaz, enough!" Abba's face drained of color, and he squeezed his eyes shut, his jaw muscle dancing.

Ahaz glared at their cousin Isaiah. How dare he use this wedding as leverage to push the prophets' agenda. Since Yahweh struck Saba Uzziah with leprosy when he tried to offer his own sacrifice, many Judeans had been too frightened to worship in Yahweh's Temple—including the king and prince.

Abba took a deep breath, opened his eyes, and raised his chin. "It's not like we don't worship Yahweh, Isaiah. We simply choose to make our sacrifices elsewhere."

"You mean on the high places." Isaiah stepped closer to the dais, challenging the king. "On the same altars people make sacrifices to Molech and Chemosh and Baal."

Jotham's eyes narrowed. "You have no proof they worship other gods on the high places."

"The prophets' words are proof enough, Cousin. And the Law requires that sacrifices to Yahweh be made *only* at the Temple where His presence dwells." Isaiah stepped back, took his wife's hand, and repeated his demand. "We humbly request that the royal household attend a sacrifice at Yahweh's Temple on the day of Ahaz and Abijah's wedding."

Request. Hah! Ahaz boiled inside, watching his abba contemplate Isaiah's *demand.* Finally, the king turned his gaze to the young couple. "Ahaz, my son, you will rule this kingdom one day and make many difficult decisions."

His expression softened when he addressed the beautiful young woman at Ahaz's side. "Abijah, as queen, you will also make hard choices that will test your loyalties to husband, family, nation, and faith. I will leave this decision to the two of you to work out. A sacrifice should be made on your wedding day—you must decide together if it occurs at the Temple or on a high place."

Abijah's grip tightened, and Ahaz gently loosened her fingernails from his forearm as he led her a few steps away from Isaiah and Aya. "I know you want to please your guardians, Abijah, but have you seen what Yahweh did to my saba?"

She nodded, her beautiful black eyes filling with tears. "Yes. King Uzziah lived in a rented house outside the walls of Tekoa. I saw him occasionally." She looked down and scrubbed at the calluses on her hands. "But my abba is the high priest, your majesty. He would be so honored to offer a sacrifice at the Temple on our wedding day."

Ahaz brushed her cheek, imagining how it might look with the same leprous lesions he'd seen on Saba Uzziah's face. Quiet fury rose in his belly as he tilted her chin up and stared into her eyes. "I can't—I won't—take the chance that we will somehow displease Yahweh. Saba was faithful to the LORD his whole life, and look what happened to him."

"But Abba said King Uzziah broke the Law when he tried to enter the sanctuary. Only the high priest is allowed—"

"And what do you think Yahweh would do to the likes of me?" Ahaz's voice echoed in the near-empty hall, and Abijah's wide eyes betrayed her fear.

The prince dropped his hands, straightened his robe, and regained his composure. "I won't risk your life or mine by visiting the Temple. We'll find another way to involve your abba in our wedding."

Only a slight hesitation preceded her nod. "Of course, your majesty. Whatever you think best."

He pulled her into a tender hug. "I will always do what I think is best for you, Abijah. Always."

NINE

"Ahaz was twenty years old when he became king, and he reigned in Jerusalem sixteen years. Unlike David his father, he did not do what was right in the eyes of the Lord his God."

2 Kings 16:2

5 Years Later

Ahaz sat on a cushioned bench beneath a large canopy sipping honeyed wine and watching a team of oxen strain against their yoke. Renovations on the Temple's Upper Gate were painfully slow.

"Careful, now!" Shouted the foreman. Another hewn stone —the size of a ram, the weight of a horse—hung in the air, suspended by braided hemp ropes and tied to the straining oxen. "Pull that block to the right." Two men stood precariously, waiting to seat the stone atop a bed of soft mortar.

"Drive the oxen forward. Just a little." The foreman shouted at the farmer, who used his goad to prod his team. "Stop! Stop!" Sweat dripped into the foreman's eyes. "Perfect! Now, move them back, and seat the stone."

Ahaz held his breath, watching, as one more stone was set in place. The ropes went slack, and the weight of the stone squeezed the excess mortar from between the massive blocks. A cheer rose, and the foreman cast a satisfied glance over his shoulder at Ahaz, who nodded his approval.

This was Ahaz's contribution to construction projects: drinking wine and nodding. What did he know of pulley systems, quarrying stones, and masonry? His talents were displayed with sword and spear. Ahaz had led Judah's army to victory against all their enemies and collected more foreign tribute than Judah's treasury had seen since the days of Solomon. But now peace ate at Ahaz's gut like rancid meat. *What I wouldn't give for another war.*

"Your majesty." A royal messenger knelt at his feet, interrupting his thoughts. "King Jotham requests your presence in the Throne Hall."

"Hmm." A grunt was all he could muster. What had he done wrong this time? Ahaz hoped when he'd been crowned co-regent last month, Abba would stop treating him like a child. Ahaz was twenty years old with a wife and two children, but Abba still commanded him.

The messenger remained on his knees, adding to Ahaz's irritation. "Get up. Let's go." The boy fairly leapt to his feet and hurried toward the Temple's Upper Gate, but Ahaz shouted, "Not through there, you idiot!"

Still reluctant to enter even the public courts of Yahweh's Temple, Ahaz led the messenger through the city streets toward the main entrance of the palace. Many royal guards who had served in Ahaz's military campaigns saluted him and shared knowing grins. His men were a special breed, loyal to him alone, sharing secrets of their service that only Judeans of like mind ever needed know.

After long days of battle, they'd spent their nights around campfires. Ahaz told the stories of foreign gods Dannah taught him as a child—and then rewarded his men with the priestesses of those gods after they conquered foreign nations. When his men returned to Judah, they discovered their surrounding hillsides were covered with high places and altars—even the priestesses were available if they knew where to look. Ahaz made sure his men could continue their worship, and they worshiped with fervor. Thankfully, King Jotham remained oblivious to it all.

Ahaz reached the courtroom, and the guards opened the double doors as Judah's co-regent approached. The Throne Hall was unusually quiet. Why would Abba cancel court proceedings today? Ahaz heard the tell-tale sounds of his two-year-old son inside and, when he reached the threshold, saw that his wife, their two sons, and King Jotham awaited his arrival. He felt as if one of the Temple stones had landed in his gut.

His wife, Abijah, faced the throne, her back to the door, holding their newborn, Hezekiah. She didn't turn to greet him.

Their firstborn, Bocheru, played happily with the king's scepter until he saw Ahaz approach. "Ah-bah?" His tender brow furrowed; his smile disappeared; and he hurried toward Abijah, clinging to her leg.

"Come, Ahaz," Abba said, his voice sharp as a sword. Then, he addressed the guards. "Everyone may leave us. All of you, please."

Ahaz waited at the back of the room, cooling his temper and gathering his wits before managing his abba's anger. How dare Abijah involve the king in their argument from this morning? Evidently, King Jotham was taking her side.

Inhaling a determined calm, Ahaz marched forward when the last guard shut the door behind him. "Bocheru, come and see your abba." He opened his arms, hoping to continue building the relationship. The boy hardly knew him since Ahaz had been fighting wars for most of Bocheru's short life.

Abijah nodded at their son and dislodged him from her legs. Bocheru walked haltingly to his abba. Ahaz scooped him up and continued to his wife's side, laying his arm around her shoulders. When he pulled her close to kiss her forehead . . . .

He noticed the bruise on her left cheekbone and the dark, red circle under her eye. He felt as if his heart melted in his chest. "Abbi, I . . ." Then he shot a pleading glance at his abba. "I didn't . . ."

"You didn't what, Ahaz?" Jotham's face was crimson, his voice shaking. "Are you really saying you didn't do this to your wife?"

"No, I . . ." Ahaz turned back to Abijah. "I didn't think I hit you that hard."

She choked on a humorless laugh that erupted more like a sob. Covering her mouth, she regained control and turned to King Jotham. "Is it acceptable that your son hit me at all?"

Before he could answer, Ahaz grabbed her arm and whirled her to face him. "Abbi, I didn't mean to hurt you." The baby in her arms began wailing, so Ahaz spoke above the noise. "I may have had a little too much wine this morning, but honestly—all you've done since I returned home from battle is complain. You say I don't spend enough time with Bocheru, and when I try to play with him, you say I'm doing it wrong."

"You're too rough with him!"

"He's a boy, Abbi. He needs to learn toughness!"

"Enough!" The king stood, towering over them on his dais. He glared down at his son. "Your wife sent her maid to request this audience and entered this courtroom through the servant's halls so she wouldn't be seen. She has used discretion in reporting your abuse—"

"Abuse?" Ahaz blustered. "I barely touched her."

Jotham lifted his hand for silence. "You will not 'touch her' again, Ahaz. Do you hear me? A king is to provide an example for the people of Judah."

Ahaz held his tongue, refusing to acquiesce or argue. He

was co-regent of Judah—equal to King Jotham in power if not in popularity. He need not bow ever again.

In the awkward silence, Jotham descended the six steps, meeting Ahaz face-to-face. "You are co-regent, my son, and you have secured the loyalty of many soldiers, but the hearts of the Judean people still belong to me. Dannah is too old to bear another son, but I will marry again and give your throne to another if you continue to defy me. Don't think I won't." He leaned closer, whispering so only Ahaz could hear. "You will treat Abijah with respect and discontinue your reckless pursuit of pagan prostitutes. Is that clear?"

He stepped back, holding his son's gaze. With barely controlled rage, Ahaz nodded once. "You've made yourself abundantly clear." If King Jotham wished to cross political swords, Ahaz was up to the challenge. War—of any kind—was much more to his liking than stacking blocks at Yahweh's Temple.

He placed his hand at the small of Abijah's back. "Come, my dear. Let's return to our upstairs chamber. I'll take the rest of the day to be with you and the children." His false smile felt more like a lion bearing his teeth, and the fear in Abijah's eyes confirmed it.

The royal family returned to their private chamber in silence, the guards at their door bowing as they entered. Two nursemaids appeared from the adjoining servants' chamber and removed Ahaz's sons without a word, leaving him alone with his beautiful, trembling wife. His anger dissolved like horse dung in the rain.

Her head was bowed. He stepped closer, reaching for her, but she stepped back. "Ahaz, no. Please. Let me say what I need to say."

"Alright." He tamped down his annoyance.

"We are married because of Yahweh, because He declared our match in Aya's dreams when I was a baby." She looked up then, her eyes pleading. "Perhaps our relationship has been weakened because I've started worshiping Asherah with you."

Ahaz took two large strides and cradled his wife's face, covering her lips with a kiss. He couldn't let her return to the prim and proper Yahweh priest's daughter he'd married. He felt her relax into his arms, and he looked down into her eyes. "Yahweh may have foretold our marriage through Aya, but even your high-priest abba would agree—we all have a choice of which gods we serve."

PART IV

UNEXPECTED TREASURE –
YAIRA'S STORY

TEN

*"The word of the Lord that came to Micah of Moresheth
during the reigns of Jotham, Ahaz and Hezekiah, kings of
Judah."*
Micah 1:1

(Two Years Before Ahaz Becomes Co-Regent) — Between Moresheth and Bethlehem — Yaira

Yaira repositioned herself on the donkey, trying to make her left leg stop tingling. "Micah, how much longer till we reach Bethlehem?"

Her brother looked over his left shoulder, frustration crinkling his brow. "Don't ask again. I told you when we stopped for our midday meal that we'd be there before sunset. Has the sun set?"

She pouted her bottom lip and studied her hands. Micah had been cranky with her ever since Ima and Abba . . . .

The donkey stopped its plodding, and Micah's hands came to rest on Yaira's legs. "Look at me, little sister." When she refused, he tipped up her chin. His eyes were ringed with dark circles, and muddy tear streaks stained his cheeks. "I'm sorry I was cross. You're only seven years old and have never traveled before. I should be more patient."

Well, now she felt like a baby. She folded her arms across her chest. "I'm fine. Keep going."

He cupped her cheek in his hand. "I miss Ima and Abba too. I'm sorry I was at the prophet's camp in Tekoa when the Philistines attacked." He dropped his hand and bowed his head, sniffling. "I should have been there to protect you, to protect them." He wiped his nose on his sleeve.

People stared as they passed by on the merchant's road toward Bethlehem. Yaira patted his shoulder. "Why can't you take me back to the prophet's camp with you? Please, Micah. I'll be good. I won't complain. I'll learn to cook and sew and—"

He wiped his face and looked up at her. "I can't take care of you, Yaira. You'll be fine in Bethlehem with Master Abraham and his wife. They're expecting their first child, and you'll be a wonderful handmaid to Mistress Esli."

"Please, Micah. I don't want to live with strangers. I want to live with you."

His face grew stern, and she wished she hadn't argued. "You're too young to understand, Yaira, but serving in Master Abraham's household is your best chance at a normal life. You'll see. Someday, you'll meet a man, marry, and have beautiful babies I can bounce on my knee."

Yaira's final plea came from the deepest sorrow of her heart. "So I lose my parents to a Philistine raid and my big brother to Yahweh's prophets within a few days?"

Micah raised a single brow. "You'll make a fine ima someday. You weave guilt the way a weaver works the loom." He kissed the tip of her nose and started walking again, calling over his shoulder. "No more complaining. We'll be in Bethlehem soon."

True to his word, Micah led them to the walled village well

before sunset. As they approached, he hailed the judges seated at the southern gate. "Shalom, brothers. I'm looking for Abraham ben Obadiah."

They pointed toward a fine-looking two-story stone house connected to the outer wall of the city. Micah led the donkey toward the door, but slowed as they heard a woman shouting inside.

"I'm not without compassion, Abraham. I'm sorry for the orphaned girl, truly, but how will I care for a seven-year-old child when I can barely care for myself?"

Then a man's voice. "You won't need to care for her, Esli. We're taking her in so she can become your handmaid. She'll learn to cook, to clean, to spin, weave—all the things you do."

"And who will teach her, Abraham? You? I'm nine-month's pregnant and can barely care for myself. I'm swollen from head to toe and can't even bend over to lace my sandals!"

"Esli, they'll be here any minute—" It was then that Master Abraham stepped into the doorway and saw Micah and Yaira. His face turned the color of goat's milk. "Um . . . er, uh . . . welcome." He tried to smile, but Yaira couldn't. She wasn't willing to pretend.

Micah stepped toward the doorway and looked inside. "I won't let my sister be a burden, Mistress Esli. I'll gladly take her to the prophet's camp in Tekoa until other arrangements can be made for her well-being. I'm sorry to have inconvenienced you."

Master Abraham grabbed his arm. "No, Micah. Please." He glanced over his shoulder at his wife. "I should have better prepared Esli for Yaira's arrival. My wife is in desperate need of help, and I know your sister will be a great blessing to our household." He met Yaira's frightened gaze. "And I believe we can be a blessing to you too, little one. We want you to be a member of our family, not just a servant. Please, Yaira." He lowered his voice as if sharing a secret, but he still spoke loud enough for the mistress to hear. "My wife is sort of cranky at first, but she grows on you after a while."

"Abraham!" Mistress shouted from inside.

Yaira giggled in spite of her fear but covered her smile right away and looked at Micah. *What will you do?* He'd made it clear on the way here that she wasn't in charge of her future.

Micah turned from Yaira's pleading gaze and addressed the woman inside the house. "I leave the decision to you, Mistress Esli. Does Yaira stay and become your handmaid, or do I take her to Tekoa and look for another household in which she can serve?"

Yaira heard a shuffling of sandals and then saw a woman appear in the doorway—the most beautiful, most *pregnant* woman she'd ever seen. Mistress Esli inspected Yaira from head to toe, and the girl wished she'd had a chance to at least wash her face beforehand.

When the woman grimaced, Yaira felt certain she would be going to Tekoa, and a piece of her heart rejoiced. But when the woman's grimace turned to a groan, and she doubled over in pain, Yaira realized the mistress' laboring had begun.

Master Abraham led his wife toward their bed chamber and called over his shoulder. "Micah, you and your sister fetch the midwife. Yaira, welcome to our family!"

ELEVEN

"God sets the lonely in families."
Psalm 68:6

"One more strong push, Esli, and your baby will be here." The midwife crouched between Esli's knees, holding a clean blanket. Yaira sat on a stool behind her new mistress, who was perched over birthing stones.

"You can do it, Mistress. One more push." Yaira had never been so exhausted. Nor had she ever felt this kind of excitement. She had labored with her new mistress for nearly two days. They'd cried together, laughed a little. She'd rubbed the woman's back and feet with scented oils. Now—in just moments—a new little life would enter this world.

Yaira leaned over Mistress Esli's shoulder and pressed her cheek against the woman's face. "We'll push together." She pressed forward, while the mistress grabbed her knees and grew red-faced with the effort. With the final attempt came a gush of squalling new life.

"It's a girl!" The midwife caught the babe in the blanket.

Yaira released Mistress Esli, gently resting her back against the stool. She watched in wonder as the midwife tended to Esli's post-birth needs and then rubbed the baby with salt and wine. The crying infant, intent on trying out her lungs, protested as her skin pinked with the gentle scrubbing. Finally, wrapped and quiet, the little one was placed in Yaira's arms while the midwife helped Mistress onto the sleeping mat beside the birthing stones. Once Esli was settled, she opened her arms, and Yaira offered the baby girl to her ima for the first feeding. The contented sound of suckling brought a smile to three weary faces.

Looking up from her new baby, the mistress called Yaira to sit beside her. "I must ask forgiveness for the things you over-heard when you and Micah arrived. My husband's wisdom has often proven beyond my understanding and such was true when he brought you into our lives, Yaira." She pulled the girl close and kissed her forehead. "I'll never be able to repay the blessing you've already shown me."

"You need not repay me, Mistress." Yaira bowed her head, unable to speak past the lump in her throat, and determined to hide her tears on this joyful day.

Mistress tilted up her chin. "I'm so sorry about your parents, little one, and I know you miss them terribly." Yaira nodded. Esli searched her eyes as if looking for a hidden treasure. "Do you know that sometimes our greatest blessing emerges from desolation?"

Yaira shook her head, not sure that she understood the word. "Desolation?"

"*Desolation.* It's like a barren land, where nothing can grow. It's a feeling of forsakenness, abandonment, with seemingly no hope."

"I suppose I know desolation well. I just never knew what it was called."

The mistress' eyes misted. "But remember what I said? Sometimes great blessing comes from that desolation." She looked down at her new baby. "This little one will help you forget your desolation, Yaira. She is mine but also yours. You helped bring her into this world, and you'll help raise her."

Yaira's breath caught as she stroked the baby's downy-soft head. "I thought I was to be your handmaid."

"You will be, but I'll also need a playmate for our daughter —and other children we might have."

"You mean, I can serve you by playing with a baby?"

The mistress laughed, wiping tears from her eyes. "Absolutely. You'll be like her big sister, and she'll be a living reminder to you that Yahweh brings life from desolation."

"Life from desolation," Yaira repeated as she leaned down to kiss the baby's head.

Mistress Esli brushed Yaira's cheek. "We'll call our girl *Ishma—Desolation*. She'll be full of life and joy, reminding us that Yahweh can make even our darkest days shine like the sun."

The door scraped across the packed dirt floor. "Did I hear a baby crying?" Master Abraham poked his head inside. When he glimpsed his wife and baby, he rushed across the room and fell to his knees beside them. He kissed them both and even pecked Yaira's forehead with a kiss. "I'm so proud of all of you."

"Meet your new daughter," the mistress said. "Her name is Ishma."

"Desolation?" His brows knit together.

But before he could criticize, Mistress Esli explained. "It's a lesson for Yaira—for us all—that out of desolation comes Yahweh's most precious gifts."

They exchanged a glance that Yaira couldn't quite decipher. She appreciated Mistress Esli's effort to teach an important lesson, but naming a child *desolation* seemed a dangerous way to go about it. Yaira knew a girl named Joel—*mountain goat*—and the boys always made goat sounds and laughed at her skinny legs. Yaira knew a boy named Gideon—*warrior*—who was constantly fighting with both his enemies and friends. Would this little girl named *desolation* live out its meaning for the rest of her life?

"Yaira?" Master Abraham said. "Did you hear me?"

She felt her cheeks warm. "I'm sorry, Master, no." She stood quickly and bowed. "How may I serve you?"

His features softened, and he laid his arm around her shoulders. "No, Yaira. It is I who wish to serve you." He guided her toward a ladder and pointed toward a second story. "I've taken the bundle of things you brought from home upstairs in your room. It's time you got some rest."

Yaira looked over her shoulder at Mistress Esli. "But what if she needs—"

"You get some sleep." I'll care for Esli and the baby for a while. "When you feel rested, we'll show you what other chores will be asked of you. Go on now."

Tentatively, she climbed the ladder, looking back at the mistress with each step. Would she change her mind and wish Yaira gone by the time she woke? As she laid down on a straw mat and rested her head on a piece of lamb's wool, Yaira wrestled with more questions chasing each other in circles around her mind.

Would the baby be all right? The midwife said she was healthy, but Yaira heard babies sometimes died for no reason at all. When Abba and Ima died, did they just go into darkness, or did they live somewhere else? Would she ever see them again?

An overwhelming yawn nearly swallowed her face, and she snuggled onto her side, closing her eyes against the afternoon sun. When she woke, she would help fix the evening meal. When she woke, she would prove her worth to both Master and Mistress. When she woke, perhaps she could hold little Ishma again . . . .

TWELVE

"Give ear, our God, and hear; open your eyes and see
the desolation . . .We do not make requests of you because
we are righteous, but because of your great mercy."
Daniel 9:18

Yaira stirred the pot of lentils and added half-a-pitcher
of water so the stew could cook a while longer without
sticking. She'd been helping her ima in the kitchen since
she was five and knew three recipes by heart. Simple wheat
bread, the staple of every Judean household. Gruel with a little
honey for morning meals. And lentil stew with onions and
garlic to satisfy evening hunger.

The first week's lunches had been goat cheese, olives, dates,
and whatever fresh produce Master Abraham brought home
from the market. The women of Bethlehem had helped supple-
ment their sparse menu by sharing offerings from their own
tables when they came to visit Mistress and little Ishma.

Only a few careless remarks had been made about the baby's
name, but Mistress Esli responded with what Yaira learned was
her usual silk-covered brick. "Abraham and I believe it's not the

name that makes the child but the child that makes the name."
She smiled sweetly at a woman named Abana. "Surely, your
parents would never have named you *Made of Stone* had they
not believed you could soften a heart."

Abana smiled just as sweetly, placed her kettle of lamb stew
on the table and wished the mistress good day before scurrying
out the door. Yaira tried not to giggle, but failed miserably.

On the morning of Ishma's eighth day, Mistress met Yaira as
she climbed down the ladder at dawn. "I'm tired of watching
you do all the work, Yaira. It's time I resumed my household
duties." Her eyes looked tired but determined. Master Abraham
had already gone to sit in his judge's seat at the city gate. There
would be no arguing with the mistress.

Without a word, Yaira hurried back up the ladder and
returned with a sling she'd fashioned for the woman. "This is
my gift for you and the baby." She ducked her head. "I suppose
it's not a real gift since Master Abraham purchased the cloth,
but I sewed the ends together to make an infant sling. Here. Let
me show you."

She slipped it over Esli's head and under one arm, and then
wrap it twice around her waist to keep the baby safe and warm.
"See? It will hold Ishma against your chest so you can nurse or
simply keep her close enough that she can hear your heartbeat
while she sleeps. My ima always gave a sling to the new imas in
our village."

Mistress' face lit up as if Yaira had given her all the gold in
Judah. "A few of the women in Bethlehem have these, but I
never knew how they worked." She kissed the top of Yaira's
head. "Thank you, love. Let's grind some grain and see how
Ishma likes it."

The baby slept while Mistress Esli and Yaira worked
together all morning. They ground grain, baked bread, and
spun wool, talking of Yaira's parents, the Philistine raid, and
Micah.

"He's much older than me," Yaira said, standing and twirling her spindle beside Mistress' stool.

The woman looked up, brows furrowed. "Did your parents ever say why there were so many years between you?"

"Ima said she nearly died giving birth to Micah, and the midwife told her she might never have another child. She always called me her unexpected treasure." Yaira smiled at the memory despite the heartache. Oh, how she missed her ima.

"She sounds like a lovely woman. I wish I could have met her." Mistress gazed down at baby Ishma, and Yaira was happy for the silence. Sometimes she just wanted to think and not talk.

"Yaira?"

She tried not to sigh. "Yes, Mistress?"

"You are my unexpected treasure too."

Tears burned Yaira's eyes. "Thank you, Mistress. I hope I don't disappoint you."

They finished their morning chores in comfortable silence. Yaira sliced some bread, a little cheese, and set out the olives, dates, and pistachios from yesterday's lunch. They heard footsteps approaching, but Yaira noted the surprise in Mistress Esli's greeting. "Well, shalom. We weren't expecting you today."

Yaira looked up and found both Master Abraham and her brother standing in the doorway. Micah's eyes were fixed on her, sadness clouding his features. "I haven't been able to stop thinking about you, little sister. How unhappy you were when I left." He turned to Esli. "I've come to take her to Tekoa. There's a family who will keep her until I can find her a permanent home."

The sound of rushing waters filled Yaira's ears, and she reached for the table to steady herself. The air in the room seemed to thicken, and she began to gasp, taking giant gulps of it.

Master Abraham swept her into his arms and carried her into his and Mistress Esli's bedchamber. When Master tried to lay her on the bed, Yaira struggled against him. "No! I can't . . . can't be . . . a bother."

"Shh, Yaira." He stood then, pulling her against his chest with a crushing hug. "Little one, you are never a bother." She felt Mistress Esli's arms surround them both, holding on so tight, little Ishma squalled her complaint from within the sling.

Yaira's breathing slowed, her panic quieting in the reassuring embrace of these people she'd come to love. She kept her face buried in the curve of Master Abraham's neck, still not able to trust her voice. Could she trust her heart? She'd only known the master and mistress for a week, but the thought of leaving them and little Ishma twisted her chest into knots.

"Please, Yaira," she heard Mistress whisper, "you are our unexpected treasure. Stay. Please stay."

Yaira lifted her head and saw *wanting* on both Master and Mistress' faces. Yes, she could trust her heart and these people. "I'll stay forever." She wrapped an arm around each of their necks and squeezed them like the lifeline they were.

Micah stood in the doorway, chuckling. "I guess I can go back to Tekoa then—alone."

Yaira squirmed in the master's arms, and he released her to run to her brother. Micah swooped her up and swung her around. They laughed as they did before the Philistine raid, before they were orphans. "I love you," she said. "Thank you for coming back for me."

He set her feet on the floor and knelt to meet her eye-to-eye. "I love you too, little one. Thank you for letting Yahweh give you a new life in Bethlehem."

Author's Note

The prophet Micah's hometown is listed in Micah 1:1 as Moresheth and associated with the Philistine-occupied city of Moresheth-Gath. Keeping in mind Israel's and Judah's constant skirmishes with the nations around them helps us remember that God's judgment on their idolatry is imminent.

The four characters you've met in the prequel, *His Unfathomable Plan*, have grown up a little in *Isaiah's Daughter*. Little Ishma is five years old when an unimaginable attack comes from the north.

> "[God gave Judah] into the hands of the king of
> Israel, who inflicted heavy casualties on
> [King Ahaz]. In one day Pekah son of
> Remaliah killed a hundred and twenty
> thousand soldiers in Judah—because Judah
> had forsaken the LORD, the God of their
> ancestors. Zikri, an Ephraimite warrior,
> killed Maaseiah the king's son, Azrikam the
> officer in charge of the palace, and Elkanah,
> second to the king. The men of Israel took

captive from their fellow Israelites who were
from Judah two hundred thousand wives,
sons and daughters. They also took a great
deal of plunder, which they carried back to
Samaria." *2 Chronicles 28:5-8*

The story of *Isaiah's Daughter* begins as Yaira and Ishma are
marched to Samaria as captives—as part of Yahweh's judgment
on King Ahaz's hard heart. Yet Ishma's story unfolds with proof
of God's faithful power to bless and protect those who remain
faithful to Him.

ADNAH'S LEGACY

PREQUEL TO ISAIAH'S LEGACY

PART I

ADNAH'S HEART –
STRIVING FOR LOVE

ONE

"[Ahaz] . . . even sacrificed his son in the fire, engaging in the detestable practices of the nations the Lord had driven out before the Israelites. He offered sacrifices and burned incense at the high places, on the hilltops and under every spreading tree."
2 Kings 16:3-4

ca. 733 B.C. — Jerusalem — Adnah

I woke to the sound of birdsong and rolled onto my back, eyes closed, feeling the prickles of my straw-filled mattress beneath me. Inhaling the cloying smells of Jerusalem's southern city through our single-window, I prayed for strength to face this day.

The sound of a wooden spoon clanged the edge of our only metal pot and launched me to my feet. "Ima, let me help," I said, bounding four paces to the cookfire. Abba was no doubt still asleep on the roof, but Ima was hard at work—as usual.

Bent over the morning's gruel, she shoved my hand away. "I'm perfectly capable—" Her words warbled like a nightingale's song and then she turned to cup my cheeks. "You will let me serve *you* on the day you're sold into servitude." Her lips pursed into a thin, white line, looking like they might burst with unspoken fury. Shaking her head, she returned to her task.

I laid my head on her shoulder and put my arm around her waist. "Don't be angry with Abba. He could have sold me to the Baal priests, but he chose a Levite's household instead." I squeezed her, hoping my next words were true. "I'm sure they're kind, and I'll be safe in Master Joseph's household."

She shrugged me away and jabbed her fists at ample hips. "Your abba doesn't deserve your mercy, Adnah. Had he not visited the Baal *priestesses* so often, he wouldn't need to sell you."

"Abba . . . " My mouth went suddenly dry. ". . . worships Baal?"

Ima swiped at her cheeks and reached for my hand. "It's time you know the truth about the men of Jerusalem."

I stiffened but let her pull me to the worn cushions in our small sitting area. I was thirteen, only one year from betrothal age. She'd already told me how a man plants his seed in a woman's belly. What else was there to know?

She tugged me down to sit on the cushion beside hers, keeping her voice low. "Men treat women as property, but we hold great power over them that they don't understand. It unnerves them. They lash out in senseless ways to prove they have authority over us. Regret then eats at their being. Makes them weak." She gathered my hands in hers, staring at me so deeply I thought she might climb into my soul. "Adnah, I love your abba, but he's not the man I once knew."

I'd seen him change too, but I thought he was devastated by King Ahaz's shocking order like the other men in Jerusalem. The king's demand of human sacrifice—firstborn sons in the fires of Molech at every new moon—had reduced even the bravest of soldiers to tears. The sacrifices would continue until Judah regained the cities lost in our most recent war.

"I think the king's pagan ways have changed everyone," I said, "but it's all the more reason the faithful among us should follow the Law. I will honor my parents, Ima, even when it means being sold to pay abba's debts." Reaching up to tuck a gray tendril behind her ear, I added, "And perhaps Master Joseph will release me after seven years as the Law dictates. Surely, the chief Levite will—"

She pressed two fingers against my lips. "You look out of those amber eyes and see the world as the Law of Moses dictates, but powerful men will see your beauty, my dove, and dictate their own law." The resignation in her voice was as if she'd seen my life already lived.

I kissed her fingers and bowed my head, acknowledging the fears of a worried ima but refusing to let myself be swept into them. *Yahweh, You know my going out and coming in. Guide and protect me as I leave my abba's household today.*

***

Shebna

The high priest, smelling of onions and stale wine, towered over fifteen-year-old Shebna but spoke to his abba. "I can't present this boy for sacrifice at the new moon, Joseph." He raked his beady eyes over Shebna's slight frame. "He isn't . . ." He scoffed, waving his hand as if shooing away a gnat and then returned to writing on his scroll. "We wouldn't present a blemished lamb to Yahweh, and King Ahaz applies the same constraints to our Molech offerings."

Blemished. Shebna wasn't even worthy to die. Shaking with fear, he felt a measure of relief, but the priest's rejection fueled the disgust in his Abba's eyes. He shoved Shebna out the door. They'd left without bowing to the high priest, but Shebna knew better than to question when Abba was angry.

Abba followed him across the temple courtyard. "Go help the women in the kitchen," he said, every step coming with another push. "You're incapable of any *real* work." Shebna stumbled over the threshold of their living quarters on the south side of temple grounds.

Their maid, Nenet, stood in the kitchen's arched doorway with Shebna's brother, Haruz. Two years younger, Haruz had always been peculiar, never capable of socializing or learning with other children.

And he was terrified of Abba. He began rocking with a low moan the moment they entered the house.

Shebna hurried over, patted his brother's shoulder. "It's all right," he whispered. "He's not angry with you." Eyes averted, Haruz nodded and hurried to his corner of the kitchen. He picked up the hand mill and resumed his favorite task— grinding grain.

"He can't even bring honor to this family by dying!" Abba shouted at Nenet.

She clamped the back of Shebna's neck, pulling him around to face Abba again. "I'll put him to work here with me, my lord." Abba turned and stormed from their living quarters.

Shebna shrugged away from her grip, rubbing what felt like bruises on his neck. "You're the servant here, Nenet, not me."

"Shall we call your abba back and ask if he values you or me most?" She searched his face in silence, and though Shebna tried to appear confident, her features softened with pity. "Let your abba spend his anger on the Levites instead of us, young master. The new housemaid came today, and we have enough work to keep us all busy." She plopped another bag of grain on the floor beside Haruz and returned to her large, wooden table to resume chopping vegetables.

Shebna's chest felt as if it was filling with thorns, and his throat clogged with panicked cries. He needed to be alone before tears came and he humiliated himself further. Grabbing a lamp from a wall niche, he raced past Nenet and threw open the wine cellar door. Fairly running down the stone steps, the cool, damp world of Abba's wineskins met his chaotic mind with row-after-row of predictability and order. His feet landed on the packed-dirt floor, and he braced his hands on his knees. Out came an agonizing groan. Then another. He crumpled to the ground, setting aside the lamp and letting his tears flow.

"Are you injured?"

The quiet voice startled Shebna to his feet. Six paces away stood a doe-eyed beauty holding a lamp. "Who are you?" His voice quaked, so he cleared his throat, trying to sound authoritative. "What are you doing in my abba's cellar?"

Lowering her head, the girl bowed. "I am Adnah, a new servant of this house." She raised her lovely face, radiating kindness. "How may I ease what pains you, my lord?"

No one had ever called him *lord,* and not since his ima died eight years ago had anyone looked at him so warmly. Without permission, his hand rose to touch her cheek.

She stepped back, her openness slamming shut.

"No, wait." Shebna pressed both arms to his sides. "Forgive me. I wanted to see if you were real."

"I assure you, I'm real." She smiled again—this time with a giggle. "And I think Nenet is testing my fortitude with the rats in this dark cellar. But I like taking inventory. A household should know what it has before determining what it needs."

I need you. His thought nearly slipped out but, thankfully, his response was more appropriate. "You're very wise, and I'm grateful you've come to our household."

Her cheeks flushed a lovely shade of pink, and the thorns in Shebna's chest were replaced by an exquisite ache. *This is the woman I will marry.*

Two

"And Ahaz took the silver and gold found in the temple of the Lord and in the treasuries of the royal palace and sent it as a gift to the king of Assyria."
2 Kings 16:8

One Year Later — Shebna

Shebna walked out of the palace and into summer's scorching heat. Tilting his face to the sky, he released a victorious shout. He took a deep breath and, smiling, began the short walk toward home as a seed of hope began to sprout. His first day in Master Isaiah's class had been like Paradise on earth. Granted, he had no right to attend since he was only a Levite, not of royal or noble blood. Abba had begged for the exception, citing Shebna's physical inadequacies as his doom unless a royal education equipped him for palace service.

Abba recited his son's failures to the teacher in the class's hearing—sent home from military training the first day and too weak for Levitical duties at the temple. At sixteen, Shebna should be earning a living and saving for marriage. Instead, he'd been relegated to learning alongside a classroom of children—and he loved it! He must pretend at least a measure of sorrow lest Abba rethink sending him to class tomorrow.

Abba's intent was to humiliate after Shebna and Haruz had failed so miserably at the temple yesterday. King Ahaz commanded every available Levite to strip the gold from all the doors, walls, and furniture, but Shebna proved too weak and Haruz, though big as an ox, couldn't tolerate the noise and confusion. Their drunken older half-brothers, born of Abba's first wife, mocked them openly and brought shame on them all. Abba sent Shebna and Haruz home. He beat Haruz for his peculiarity and begged his friend Isaiah to provide Shebna with an education so he could somehow contribute wages to their household.

Shebna had no intention of contributing to Abba's household, but he would earn wages.

And save them for Adnah's bride price.

New hope and the thought of Adnah drew him out the western city gate to the small garden plots reserved for the temple servants. Nenet always cleared the house after midday so she could rob Abba's wine cellar, often sending Shebna, Adnah, and Haruz to weed the gardens. Under the blazing sun in the deserted gardens, the three misfits had forged mighty friendships. Shebna could hardly wait to tell them about class.

His steps slowed, pondering the two people he held most dear. He was thankful Haruz would have accompanied Adnah today. A beautiful girl shouldn't wander outside the city alone. Though Haruz wouldn't hurt a lamb, he was taller than Abba with shoulders as wide as a doorframe and would provide at least the appearance of protection. Adnah seemed to enjoy his company—or at least she'd learned quickly to understand his peculiarities. Ima had taught Shebna how to calm Haruz when he grew agitated, and Adnah cared enough to learn too.

The sound of clapping captured his attention as he neared a

large rock. Climbing, he peered over the hill. Haruz sat cross-legged at the edge of a small garden plot, clapping, while Adnah stretched her arms to the sky and swayed, her long, dark hair swinging to the rhythm. Shebna held his breath, watching. Adnah danced between rows of green leaves. She dipped and leapt to Haruz's clapping. Every move filled with grace and beauty, her small frame floated effortlessly, barely touching the earth. Twirling, she opened her eyes and—

"Oh, Shebna!" Her arms fell, and she quickly sought her headscarf, cheeks flaming. "I didn't see you there."

Saddened by her discomfit, he slid off the rock and continued toward them. "Perhaps someday you'll dance for me."

Haruz met him with a hug. "Adnah likes me," he blurted. "She knows I'm smart."

Shebna patted his brother's back and released him, taking a few more steps toward the girl they both adored. "I've been gone one day, and you've discovered our secret?" He kept his tone light though the revelations made him uneasy. "Haruz must pretend to be weak of mind by remaining silent lest Abba discover he can read, write, and recite the Law and force him to earn a wage."

"But why—" Adnah stopped when Shebna gently nudged the scarf off her head and back to her shoulders.

"You need not cover your hair for me. Haruz and I know too well the need to veil ourselves." Their faces a handbreadth apart, he said, "You're too lovely to hide." Was that longing he saw? Or only his own desire reflected in her eyes?

Haruz suddenly wedged himself between them and wrapped his arms around Adnah. "I love you, Adnah."

"Haruz, stop!" Shebna shoved him aside, separating the big ox from the startled girl.

But she patted Haruz's forearm, a slight grin forming. "I'm fond of you too, my friend."

Shebna wasn't amused. "You can't hug her like that, Haruz. If anyone saw it, both yours and Adnah's reputations would be damage—" The word died with a horrifying realization. What if Nenet hoped for such a scandal to be rid of Adnah? She'd demonstrated an inexplicable hatred of the girl since Abba hired her last year, singling Adnah out for the worst tasks and criticizing her work no matter how well done.

"I'm sorry, Adnah." Haruz hung his head and dug a toe into the dirt. "Forgive me if I hugged you too hard."

"No, Haruz. You didn't hurt me." Adnah nearly impaled Shebna with a glare. "Your brother was being overly cautious."

Why was she angry with him? Couldn't she see that he was trying to protect them? And Haruz looked as if Shebna had stolen his last bite of honeyed dates. "Adnah and I know you are good, Haruz, but most people wouldn't understand your hug." He squeezed the broad shoulder of this boy in a man's body. "Remember, Ima made it my job to protect you, so trust me. It's dangerous for you to hug Adnah and tell her you love her. Please don't do it again." Ima died when Haruz was only five, but she'd taught Shebna how to speak to him simply as well as other ways to protect him, especially from Abba. Hers had been the only kindness the brothers knew—until Adnah.

"I'm sure your ima would be proud of you both." Adnah bent to resume her weeding. "When your abba returned for the midday meal, Shebna, he told us you'd been admitted to the royal classroom."

"More likely, he wondered when I'd be sent home." The words sounded more bitter than the herbs she was tending.

Haruz wrapped Shebna's shoulder and pulled him close. "He said if you failed again, he'd send you away. You can't fail, Brother. Who would protect me if he sent you away?" The fresh bruises on Haruz's arms and face proved Shebna a poor guardian.

Adnah glanced up, meeting Shebna's eyes, fresh tears glis-

tening on her lashes. Instead of the blame he expected, Shebna
saw only sadness before she returned to her task. While he'd
been at class, she must have witnessed more abuse from those
who should have loved Haruz.

Shebna pulled his brother's face close to kiss his cheek, and
then laid his head on the man-child's shoulder. "I won't fail
you, Haruz. I promise." His younger brother began rocking and
tugging at his sparse beard—signs he needed something familiar
to soothe him. Shebna knew the one thing that always worked.
"Hear, O Israel," he began and Haruz joined him, "The LORD
our God, the LORD is one . . ." His rocking slowed to the
rhythm of their words.

"You're very good with him," Adnah whispered, sitting
down beside Shebna. "He adores you."

Their shoulders touched, sending a shock like a lightning
bolt through him. "I was seven when Ima died with lung
disease. She made me promise to protect him, but I've failed
every day of my life." He was sure Adnah didn't need an explanation. A year in their household was proof enough.

"Are my sons distracting you from your work, Adnah?"
Abba's voice shattered the safety of their garden.

"They're not a distraction, my lord." Adnah fell to her
knees in the dirt. "They are gracious masters who have offered
help, but I cannot accept."

Haruz stood beside her, eyes fixed on the ground. Shebna
stepped in front of them both, empowered by his classroom
success and Adnah's encouragement. "Haruz and I will help
harvest and then carry Adnah's baskets home."

A slow grin formed on Abba's features. Then he laughed,
loud and scornful. Shebna's face burned. "If our harvest were
left in the hands of you and the imbecile, we'd all starve." His
laughter waned to a glower. "Take him back to the house and
tell Nenet I'll follow shortly with the girl."

Foreboding slid up Shebna's spine like a viper, and all color drained from Adnah's cheeks. With a slow nod and quivering smile, she said, "Tell Nenet I'll bring cucumbers and melons for tonight's meal."

Shebna hesitated, and his abba drew back his hand to strike. When Shebna didn't flinch, Abba seemed startled by his courage. Dropping his hand, he sneered, "Go, before my good mood fades."

***

Adnah

I watched Shebna and Haruz leave the garden while Master Joseph's eyes raked over me. Hating myself for allowing Shebna to nudge my headscarf to my shoulders, I lifted it again.

"No need, little Adnah," he said, his voice oddly tender. "I've had two wives but neither was as lovely as you."

He stepped closer and I moved back, nearly stumbling over the half-full basket of cucumbers. "I'm sure your wives were beautiful, my lord." I caught myself but kept my head bowed. Should I return to my work? Or would such a slight spark his wrath? He took another step and narrowed the space between us to a hand-breadth.

"My first wife was as ugly as a mule, but strong as an ox," he said, hovering over me while my head remained bowed. "Yahweh gave me three sons before she died birthing a dead baby. My older sons are Levites at the temple who bring honor to their abba."

Honor? I'd heard they were drunkards who took more than their share of the temple tax.

"My second wife was sickly and dishonored me with the two pathetic sons you know well." Tracing a line from my jaw to my chin, he tipped up my face to examine it. "Elah was lovely, and I cared for her, but my third wife will be young and beautiful, Adnah. Strong in body and spirit. I would offer her family a significant bride price, a *mohar* that cancelled any debts her abba owed me. Enough grain, wool, and oil to last them for years."

I looked away, unable to bear his eyes on me, but he continued. "I'll serve only another decade in the temple until the Law forces me to retire at age fifty. Then my five sons will provide for the needs of my household." Reaching for my hand, he trapped it between his sweaty palms. "A young wife could give me even more sons to provide for my old age—the kind of sons I deserve."

Nauseous, I stepped back and slipped my hand from his grasp. "I pray Yahweh gives you *everything* you deserve, Master Joseph." Sinking to my knees, I resumed weeding his garden. "And though I don't know your older sons, I'm certain Shebna and Haruz will honor you as the Law requires. They are good and kind men, my lord, and I'm grateful to serve in your household."

The chief Levite lingered in silence over me too long and then finally stalked away. Would my subtle rebuff make service harder in his house? Would Master Joseph approach my abba about a betrothal regardless of my implied refusal? My mind whirred so loud with questions, I didn't hear Shebna's approach.

"What did he want?" he demanded.

Frustrated by his tone, I sat back on my heels and wiped sweat from my brow. "What do you think he wanted? A submissive wife. Fat babies. And perfect sons."

His face turned crimson. "He can't have you."

Did I imagine an implied, *You're mine?* Could Shebna's bold stare mean he cared for me as I cared for him?

"Do you want to marry my abba?" he asked.

"No, I—" The relief on his face gave me courage. "I had hoped someday to marry . . . a man like *you*."

The lines between his brows softened, and his lips curved into a mischievous grin. "A man *like* me—or me?"

Bowing my head to hide the fire in my cheeks, I cursed my audacity. "It's unbecoming for a woman to invite a marriage proposal."

"You could never be unbecoming in my eyes." Shebna helped me to my feet as if I were fragile Persian pottery. He tilted up my chin, and I saw only adoration as he spoke. "You are my treasure, Adnah, and I will spend the rest of our lives together proving it."

THREE

"It is mine to avenge; I will repay.
In due time their foot will slip; their day of disaster is near
and their doom rushes upon them."
Deuteronomy 32:35

One Year Later — Adnah

"You imbecile!" Nenet ranted at Haruz, swatting him with her dish towel. "I asked for three things at the market, and you came home with one!"

"Adnah!" he cried for me, lifting his arms overhead to ward off her attack.

"I'll go!" I stepped between Haruz and the maid's wrath. "I'll be back with oil and salt before Haruz finishes grinding flour."

"Fine." Nenet squeezed my face with one rough hand. "I'll beat you with the master's strap if you're not back in time to make the dough."

She shoved me away, and I ran, praying Haruz would grind slowly and spare me a beating. Nenet's drinking had increased, and with it her violence against the two unprotected people in Joseph's household. Shebna had avoided her abuse since he was in class most days. But he received more than physical wounds from his abba when he returned home each night. No matter what topic he reported from their classroom discussions, his abba found a reason to degrade Shebna's part in it.

Stopping at the nearest market booth, I panted out, "A hin of oil and a handful of salt. Quickly, please."

"Nenet on another rampage?" The familiar merchant wagged his head. "She'll never win his heart like that."

"Whose heart?" I asked, stunned.

He placed the pitcher of oil on his counter and pressed the bundle of salt into my hand. As if planning a conspiracy, he leaned close and lowered his voice. "Nenet turned down a betrothal twenty years ago to serve in Joseph's house. All of Jerusalem knows she's wanted to be his wife these many years. No doubt, she's tired of waiting." He released my hand, his bushy black brows drawn down. "Tell the chief Levite *I'm* tired of waiting too, and I'll report him to the high priest if he doesn't pay his debt by week's end."

Too rushed to ask questions, I grabbed my purchase and raced back to temple grounds. Nenet hoped to be Master Joseph's wife? That explained her hostility when he started giving me gifts last year after his thinly-veiled proposal in the garden. I returned everything, of course, and refused his attention, reaping both his anger *and* Nenet's continued tirades.

Bursting through our back door, I bumped into the woman and knocked a full basket of dirty laundry from her arms. "Why do you still hate me?" I blurted in frustration. Her rumpled brow begged for clarity, but Haruz was hunched in the corner with his hand mill. I dared not embarrass her with such a personal discussion in front of the master's son. I grabbed her hand and pulled her outside.

Perhaps taking her into my confidence would prove I had

no feelings for Master Joseph. "I have no intention of remaining in this household when my seven years of service has ended. Shebna has already begun saving for the mohar he'll present to my abba, and we plan to move far away from Jerusalem after we marry. I'm no threat to you, Nenet."

"No threat to—" Eyes wide, her expression clouded. "Don't believe every tale you hear at the market, girl. I choose to serve Master Joseph out of loyalty. Nothing else." She grabbed my ear and pulled me back inside, pointing her bony finger too close to my face. "You'll cook every meal today while I enjoy washing a few robes with my friends at Launderer's Field. And don't you repeat any lies you've heard about me in the market."

I sniffed back tears and watched her gather the master's robes back into her basket. I'd rather cook than do laundry anyway, but her hatred withered me like killing frost on spring's first blooms. I'd offered her the most precious secret of my heart, hoping it might somehow find a crack in the thick walls she'd built to keep others away. It had been two years since I'd felt my ima's embrace, laughed with her, or shared my concerns with a woman who cared. This household was a prison holding all its members captive to their own misery.

Yahweh, free me from this place. Unlock a door so I can somehow love and be loved.

***

Shebna

Shebna hummed one of the Levite psalms, barely audible amid the noisy market. Two more pieces of silver jingled in his waist pouch, a healthy addition to the small, wooden box hidden under a floor board in the chamber he shared with Haruz. Only Adnah knew of its existence and that he regularly stayed after class each day in the marketplace, earning extra silver as a scribe. He read legal documents aloud for illiterate farmers. Wrote sales agreements. And, yes, even wrote betrothal contracts—like the one he'd pay to have written for Adnah and himself one day soon. *Not soon enough.*

Nenet's drinking and fits of rage had recently garnered Abba's notice, earning their maid a week's exile with her family in Bethlehem. She'd returned penitent in her master's presence, but more determined to make Adnah's life miserable. When Shebna came home from class one day, he found Nenet beating Adnah with Abba's strap. Immediately, he wrested away the weapon and banished Nenet to his own chamber, tending cuts and bruises on Adnah's arms. When Abba completed his temple duties that evening, Shebna related every detail, expecting justice for the young woman Abba had once thought worthy to be his wife. Instead, Shebna felt the bite of Abba's strap, and Nenet gained true authority that night. Why had he ever thought there would be justice in the chief Levite's household?

Shebna's humming ceased, silenced by the memory as he crossed the threshold of his reality. "Nenet?" Their gathering area was eerily quiet, but Nenet was almost always in the kitchen. He continued into the next room but heard none of the normal sounds. "Adnah? Haruz?" The sight of a cold hearth and tidied kitchen knocked him back a step. It looked as if no one had been here all day.

Sweat beaded on his forehead, his feet frozen to the floor. Even on the day his ima died, there was a cookfire burning. Heart beating like a drum in his chest, he turned slowly toward the closed door of his chamber, and dread crept up his legs like prickly thorns.

"It can't be," he said to no one and took his first step. "No one but Adnah knows about the box."

The possibility of his worst nightmare propelled him. Flinging his chamber door open, he halted at the threshold—

and saw his greatest fear fulfilled. A single floor panel displaced. A wooden box lay open, the lid beside it. A single scroll replacing the silver it once held. Barely breathing, Shebna took four steps and knelt beside the box. He reached for the scroll. With a trembling hand, he broke the chief Levite's wax seal and unfurled the tragic verdict. Three words. He'd known the truth of them his whole life.

You're a fool.

A guttural moan seeped through his lips as he crushed the parchment. He threw the crumpled message and released a wounded cry. "Nooo!"

A low chuckle from the doorway jolted him to his feet. Facing the mocking grin of his abba, Shebna wiped his cheeks and panted with rage. "What have you done? Where are they?"

"Did you really think you could deceive me, little weasel?"

Shebna charged the man, shrieking, "Where are Adnah and Haruz?" Like striking a brick wall, he stumbled back and looked up at the man at least a head taller.

"You sicken me," he said, sneering. "I gave Nenet to them as a wedding gift."

"You . . ." Shebna's throat closed around more words. Surely, he'd misunderstood. But Abba began to laugh, mocking Shebna's pain. Something shattered inside him, and without warning a roar erupted, and Shebna launched like a rock from a sling. Fists flying, crazed as a rabid dog, he attacked the one who had tortured him from earliest memory.

With a single blow, Abba felled him. "You are the weakest of them all," he said, looming over him, "but you will care for me in my old age as the Law commands because you are also the most ambitious."

Shebna rolled to his side and spat out blood. "You'll never touch my silver again. I'm leaving to find Adnah and Haruz."

A single kick to Shebna's abdomen refocused his attention on the face that breathed a threat. "If you leave Jerusalem or fail to provide for your abba, I will make Adnah's and Haruz's life worse than you can imagine."

Curled into a ball, gasping, Shebna felt the utter desolation of helplessness. Powerless—for now—he watched evil walk away.

"I'm hungry," Abba called over his shoulder. "You'll cook until I find a maid to replace Nenet."

Hate fueling determination, Shebna vowed silently to repay Abba for ruining his life. And someday, he'd become powerful enough to do it.

PART II

ADNAH'S LOVE –
IT'S FIRM FOUNDATION

FOUR

"In the time of Pekah king of Israel, Tiglath-Pileser king of Assyria came and took Ijon, Abel Beth Maakah, Janoah, Kedesh and Hazor. He took Gilead and Galilee, including all the land of Naphtali, and deported the people to Assyria. Then Hoshea son of Elah conspired against Pekah son of Remaliah. He attacked and assassinated him, and then succeeded him as king."
2 Kings 15:29-30

Three Days Later — Adnah

Life as I knew it was over, and words would only pour salt in the gaping wound.

The sound of ripping cloth tugged at my heavy eyelids. I rebelled at the thought of waking until I heard the ripping sound again—this time, beside my head. I bolted upright, rubbing my swollen eyes and saw Haruz tearing a strip from the bottom of his robe.

"What are you doing?" I asked in a strangled whisper. "We don't have enough silver to buy you a new robe."

We'd left Jerusalem three days ago. Master Joseph exiled us —the maid he'd never loved, the son he didn't understand, and the girl he could never have—under the protection of a hateful guard.

Haruz's hands stilled on the torn cloth, but he remained silent. He'd spoken even less than the guard since leaving Jerusalem. I could count on one hand the number of words passed between our little caravan during our journey north. On all three nights we'd camped in the wilderness, our guard Ibri communicated only with grunts, pointing, and single-word commands.

"Sleep," he said last night, before lying down with his back to us. The first night, I'd tried to talk with Nenet and Haruz, hoping to commiserate on our exile. They just shook their heads and ate their stale bread and hard cheese in lonely silence. By last night, even I had no words to waste on prattle.

Haruz tore the cloth again. I leaned over his shoulder, tugging at his arm. "What are you doing? Let me see." He pulled away but not before I saw his blistered and bleeding feet. "Oh, Haruz . . ." My throat tightened, choking off more words.

I should have noticed his wounds or at least a limp. But Haruz had lagged behind and kept to himself while we traveled. The same shame that marred his features when his abba forced us to marry still creased his brow. I reached for the cloth. "Let me help you."

"No," he said, pulling away, blocking me with his back again. "I won't have you touching my feet."

I laid a hand on his shoulder and felt his muscles tense. Realizing he didn't want to be touched, I removed my hand and sat close, hoping our friendship could outweigh the forced marriage. "Talk to me, Haruz. Are you angry? Sad? Frightened?"

He began rocking, the sign he needed reassurance only the Torah could give.

"Hear, O Israel," I whispered, "The LORD our God, the LORD is one."

Quietly, he joined my recitation. "Love the LORD your God with all your heart . . . ." We rocked together in rhythm with the words, slowing as his anxiety waned. Finally, growing still, my friend focused on the horizon. "I don't know what I feel, Adnah. Shebna always *told* me what I felt. How can I know anything without my brother to tell me?"

I'd lost my family in Jerusalem, too, but Haruz's abba and older brothers weren't as dear a loss as Shebna, the only person who truly *knew* him. "Perhaps we can learn to know things together," I said. "Can you describe how you feel now? Like I've heard you describe your feelings to Shebna."

He looked at his hands, polishing his thumbnail with nervous ambition. "My belly feels odd, but not like when Abba got angry with me." He swallowed hard and stole a quick glance at me before continuing. "When Abba yelled, my belly hurt like a thousand hornets stinging it. I could barely breathe. But now —when I look at you—the hornets turn to butterflies, and my face gets hot." Our eyes met for a moment, our faces a hand-breadth apart. "I don't like hornets or butterflies—but I like you." He returned his attention to his thumbnail. "So don't touch my feet."

I covered a grin but worked to keep any humor from my voice. "I promise not to touch your feet, but would you like to know what those hornets and butterflies mean?" He nodded. "When the hornets sting your belly, that's fear—or maybe anger. The butterflies and warm cheeks are . . ." What could I say? I'd known for over a year that Haruz cared for me deeply, but I thought Shebna would be my betrothed and Haruz would be the kind-hearted brother we'd love and protect. I felt my own cheeks grow warm at the thought of sharing a bed with this boy of fifteen—my age in years but so naïve in life. He was as tall and handsome as any man, but could he be a *husband*?

"Warm cheeks can be a good or bad feeling," I said, "depending on the circumstance."

"It's good when I think of you—and I think of you all the time."

"Well, isn't that sweet." Nenet's mocking marred the moment, her streaks of gray hair shining in pre-dawn light. "Two love-sick children can't support a household. You'd better think of ways to earn a—"

Haruz leapt to his feet and clamped Nenet's neck with one hand, nearly lifting her off the ground. "I'm the head of this new household," he said with frightening calm. "And I will no longer tolerate your cruelty, Nenet."

Face reddening, the woman gripped his wrist, eyes pleading for release.

Haruz loosened his fingers and just as quickly wrapped her in a consuming hug. "I don't want to do that again, Nenet. Please be kind to Adnah and me." Before the maid could respond, Haruz walked away and began packing his things for our final day's travel.

Nenet looked at me, her shock mirroring my own. "What did you say to him?" she asked.

"Very little." I looked at my husband with new respect, but Nenet walked away in a huff. What had been a simple yet sincere warning to Nenet had calmed many of my unspoken fears. He did realize we were to become a household, and he seemed ready to lead—at least in some ways. It would appear I had much to learn about the *man* I'd been forced to marry.

*****

1 Year Later — Jotbah, Israel

Our one-room home was within sight, but my pace slowed. I was in no hurry to deliver more bad news to my husband.

He'd worked hard on the sample contracts in my basket, but the nearby village of Jotbah was too small to require such formalities between its residents. Inhabited by as many Hittites as Israelites in the tribal territory of Zebulun, they did business with family members and long-time neighbors with little need for contracts. They also held no affection for the three Judean strangers who arrived just before harvest last year. How could we ever become more than strangers to such a segregated, tight-knit community?

When Master Joseph sent us away, our hired escort refused to disclose our destination. We never imagined we'd live among our ancestral cousins in Israel. Pagan altars and shrine prostitutes occupied every hilltop, foretelling Judah's future under King Ahaz's reign. Even those who still professed to worship Yahweh did so with a convoluted mixture of other rites and deities that held little resemblance to the faithful worship described in the Law of Moses.

Our soldier-guide chose Jotbah for its remote location and stayed only long enough to pay one-month's rent on a rat-infested, one-room house before leaving us with the clothes on our backs and two pack-mules. We sold the mules for food and supplies to last through our first winter, but we needed Haruz's writing ability to keep us from starvation.

"Perhaps he could sell copies of the Law and prophets' writings." Only twenty paces from our doorway, I chuckled at my own dark humor. Why would Jotbah want to know about Yahweh's coming judgement?

I looked at the small bag of barley in my hand and felt the blood drain from my face. How could I tell Haruz and Nenet I'd spent the last of our silver on such a small amount of grain? Perhaps I could lie, invent an order for three contracts. Haruz would believe me—until I took his completed contracts to the market and returned home without any silver. He wasn't stupid as his abba and Nenet had believed. Naïve, yes. But he was incredibly intelligent and the kindest man I'd ever known. But he was trusting to a fault.

The one and only time he'd gone to Jotbah's market alone, he came home with empty pockets, a basket of rotten vegetables, and a story about a poor widow with six children who needed the silver more than we did. The next day, we saw the "widow" in a gilded carriage with a very-alive husband. Haruz understood the warm cheeks of embarrassment, and we salvaged a few vegetables for two days of watery stew. Though I still adored his tender heart, I had to agree with Nenet. Haruz must never again go to the market alone.

"Yahweh, be our Provider," I whispered, pushing aside the worn curtain to enter our home.

Nenet stood beside the cookfire, stirring something in our metal pot. Haruz was bent over a potsherd, writing something with mud and a sharpened twig. Nenet looked up first. I tried to greet her with a hopeful smile. Nenet's face paled, and I knew I'd failed.

Haruz wasn't as adept at reading expressions. "How many contracts did you sell?" he asked, finally looking up from his writing project.

"None!" Nenet shouted, tossing her wooden spoon into the pot. "How will we eat this winter if we can't buy grain?" Tears started down her cheeks, as her shouts turned to hysteria. "My life wasn't supposed to be this way. Why—"

Haruz leapt to his feet and engulfed her in a ferocious hug. "I'll go to the village myself and show people how well I write."

"No!" Nenet shoved him away and then looked at me. "Tell him. You must tell him why he can't go."

Haruz's dark brows drew down, glancing over me to the packed-dirt floor. "I'm a man and your husband, Adnah, not an imbecile."

"Of course, you're not an imbecile." I stepped toward him, but he retreated. Anger warred with hurt, raising an army of emotion that cut off my words. Only Nenet had received his hugs since arriving in Jotbah. When we left Jerusalem, I wondered if I could accept him as a husband. I'd never considered he might reject me as his wife.

Bowing my head to hide tears, I worked to keep my voice from shaking. "Why won't you let me touch you?"

"I'm going to the village with you tomorrow," he said, ignoring my question.

My head snapped up as he turned his back and crossed his arms. "Nenet," I said between clenched teeth, "leave us alone please." If he wanted to be a husband, he must treat me as a wife.

She stormed past us. "He's not going to the village, Adnah. Don't you let him talk you into it." Closing the curtain behind her, the silence widened the chasm between us.

I ached to place my hands on his well-muscled back, but instead I whispered, "Haruz, will you sit down with me?" I sat at his feet and patted the packed dirt beside me.

Slowly, stiffly, he sat. Stared at the wall. An arm's length between us.

"Am I unattractive to you, Husband?"

His head snapped in my direction, eyes meeting mine for only a moment before a glimmer of pain took his gaze away. He grabbed his wild mop of dark hair and rocked furiously. "I don't know how to be a husband, Adnah. I'm trying to obey Shebna, and I don't want to hurt you."

"Obey Shebna? Hurt me?" I pulled his hands from his hair. "How are you obeying Shebna?" He pulled his hands away and kept rocking.

I thought we had left Jerusalem while Shebna was in class. Had Shebna somehow known his abba would send us away and given Haruz instructions before we left?

"When we were in the garden," Haruz interrupted my thoughts, his words rushing out in a torrent. "Shebna said I shouldn't hug you. It could damage you. I can hug Nenet. She's a tough old bird. But not you. You're soft. Tender. What if I break you?"

I covered a laugh that escaped like a sob.

He stopped rocking. Shocked. "Are you mocking me?"

"Not at all, Haruz!" Horrified, I rushed to explain. "Shebna warned you when we were *friends* that your hugs could damage my reputation." *And when* he *was to be my betrothed.* "But we're married now, and—" I leaned over and slipped my arms around his neck. "I won't break, Haruz. A wife needs her husband's touch."

He swallowed hard and tentatively slid one arm around my waist. Strong, yet tender, the warmth of his touch sent longing through me in waves.

I pulled myself into his lap, curling my arms around his head and burying my face in the bend of his neck. "Hold me, Haruz. Please, hold me."

He began rocking again, this time slowly and rhythmically. His hand drew gentle circles on my back. He began exploring my shoulders, the length of my arm, and then each finger, studying me with wonder. When he lifted his head, I brushed my lips across his and his breath caught. A spark in his eyes turned to a flame.

Breathing labored, he turned away and whispered, "How could you ever love a man like me?"

I pressed my forehead against his, longing for a real kiss. "Haruz ben Joseph, I believe we can love each other as husband and wife—if you'll allow it."

He sighed. I hoped it was relief. "You must teach me." His tone was timid, defeated.

I lifted his face between my hands to peer into his soft-brown eyes. "We will teach each other—as it should be."

FIVE

"The king of Assyria invaded the entire land [of Israel],
marched against Samaria and laid siege to it . . ."
2 Kings 17:5

5 Years Later — Jerusalem — Shebna

"Assyrian troops laid siege to Samaria overnight," Isaiah explained to the class, eliciting the expected gasps from Judah's high-born children. "Yahweh's judgment has begun against Israel's capital as His prophets have prophesied for years."

Shebna heard the news on his way to the palace this morning, and as assistant tutor, he should have explored the lesson on foreign relations. Isaiah, however, insisted the event fell under *religion*, so Shebna acquiesced, giving the head tutor some credit for being the only Yahweh prophet brave enough to remain in Jerusalem.

"The prophet Micah told of their coming destruction years ago . . ." Isaiah blathered on about his fellow prophets, men hiding like rats because of King Ahaz's threats. Isaiah was the king's cousin and was safe from execution—for now.

Why couldn't these Yahwists accept that Judah was moving into the future, shedding the chains of their past? Even the priests and Levites had accepted the new altar King Ahaz commissioned—an exact replica of Assyria's altar—in Yahweh's temple courts. Why must the prophets be so intolerant?

"They've arrested King Hoshea and *started* a siege against Israel's capital city," Shebna emphasized the facts when he grew tired of Isaiah's propaganda. "Judean spies say Samaria can last for years within the high walls, so Judah's troops are preparing for Assyrian frustrations to filter into our northern villages."

A bright nobleman's son raised his hand. "We must, of course, protect our northern villagers, but isn't it dangerous for Judah to oppose any Assyrian troops? We don't need to bring down Shalmaneser's wrath on us."

"True," Shebna replied, "but we dare not leave our northern brethren unshielded. The only thing Assyria hates more than betrayal is cowardice. Judah will protect her own." Even as Shebna spoke the words, his spine straightened with pride. Prince Hezekiah, his friend and past classmate, had trained for war and would soon lead his own battalion to battle the Philistines on Judah's southwest border. Though Abba never let Shebna forget that he was too small and weak to carry a sword, preparing these young leaders was a privilege Shebna took seriously.

By midday, Isaiah's incessant ranting about Yahweh's coming judgment showed no sign of dwindling, and Shebna's patience had worn thin. "Class dismissed!" Shebna announced without warning. "Use the rest of this day to gather opinions from your parents and other adults in the Upper City about how the Assyrians' invasion of Israel will affect Judah—and Jerusalem in particular."

As the students scurried from the room, Shebna tried to

ignore the seething glare from his head tutor. "Is it so difficult for you to admit that Yahweh is at work," he asked Shebna.

While gathering a few scrolls, and his box of reeds and pigments into a shoulder bag, Shebna chuckled and feigned indifference. "Yahweh is always at work, Master Isaiah." Meeting his tutor's eye, he let a fraction of the truth slip out in his tone. "But as long as King Ahaz gives Judeans a choice to see other gods working as well, Yahweh will need to work a little harder."

Isaiah's shocked expression was his only answer, and Shebna left the classroom in the sweet silence of victory. Walking through the palace, he drew his shoulders back and chin up. Isaiah, no longer a member of the king's council or revered royal family, was now just a fanatic Yahweh prophet. Shebna may be only the assistant royal tutor, but for the first time in his life, he'd tasted power over a superior, and it was sweeter than his first candied date. Isaiah would never report Shebna's behavior to his cousin, King Ahaz, which meant Shebna could teach whatever he wished. Do whatever he wanted.

The heady promise of new freedom carried him home on a cloud of anticipation. He barely noticed his abba's presence in the front room when he entered their home. Barely heard him speak until a shout garnered his attention.

"Did you hear?" Abba stood in front of him, panting. Not angry—frightened.

"No, Abba, I . . . What?"

"The Assyrians! They've invaded Israel." He shook Shebna's shoulders. Searched his face. Then looked deep into his eyes as if falling into them. "I should never have sent them there."

"Sent who—"

Abba staggered back, catching himself on the edge of a table. He lowered himself to a cushion, but spoke as to the air. "I sent Ibri a week ago to find out why Haruz stopped sending silver."

The confession knocked the air from Shebna's lungs, and with it he whispered her name. "Adnah."

Abba looked up, a sneer affixed on his dusky-white face. "Yes, and Haruz and Nenet. All three in a small Israelite village. But the guard who knew their exact location hasn't returned."

Shebna lunged at him, grasping the front of his robe. "Why didn't you get them out of Israel when you knew the Assyrians were coming?"

Abba swatted at his hands. "Haruz scribes for a living, and I thought the Assyrians would pay well for his service." He looked away with sort of a pouting frown. But Shebna knew him too well. It was defeat that sobered him, not shame.

The timid girl Abba had married peeked around the corner, a fresh bruise on her left cheekbone. "Welcome home, Master Shebna. May I bring you a cup of watered wine?"

She was the only one left that Abba could bully. "No, thank y—"

"There'll be no more wine for anyone if Shebna is the only one bringing me silver." Abba's words were slurred, having already sampled too much of the wine in his cellar. After Nenet left with the mismatched newlyweds, Abba lived in a drunken stupor. He was too wicked to feel regret and too selfish to feel lonely. Did he miss Adnah, Shebna's beloved that he'd once hoped to marry?

His drunken antics cost him his role as chief Levite; and with Abba no longer in authority to protect them, Shebna's elder brothers were quickly discharged as well. Now, the only one earning a wage was Shebna. At least, that's what he believed —until today.

He leaned over this weakened old man and worked to maintain his patience. "Did anyone accompany Ibri to check on Haruz?" Ibri was an old temple guard—also discharged for dishonorable behavior—who Abba called on to do odd jobs.

"No," he grunted. "Ibri works alone. Always has."

"And when did my brother *start* sending you silver?"

Abba lifted his hand, as if to strike. Shebna flinched, a reflex, but he quickly raised his chin, the memory of his victory over Isaiah fueling his confidence. "Listen, old man. I'm the only one standing between you and the streets. Where are Adnah and Haruz, and when did they start sending you silver?"

The old Levite's lips curved into a thin-lipped grin. "They're in one of the northernmost villages of Israel. I started receiving silver wrapped in a leather-covered scroll from your brother two years ago. It always arrived with the same Hittite merchant who traveled to Jerusalem once-a-month. He said it came from a man who was big as an ox, silent as a stone, with a wife as beautiful as the angels."

Shebna felt his chest constrict as if crushed by a vice. How could the mere mention of Adnah still cause such pain?

A low chuckle refocused his attention, and he found Abba's rheumy eyes fixed on him. "You were a fool to think such a beauty would ever care for you," he said. "I did you a favor by sending her away."

The man before him was viler than he could imagine, but Joseph ben Abidan was his inescapable responsibility. If any noblemen of Judah heard he'd abandoned his Abba, Shebna would be ostracized. He must live behind a veil until he attained real power, the kind of power that could truly change his life. For now, he would tend to Abba's needs—and the prospect of it tightened like chains around his throat.

"As you have done for me," he whispered, "I will favor you by finding Haruz and ensuring his safety—so you'll have your wine and your silver, Abba." Indeed, he would use every contact he had in the palace to find Ibri and the village where his brother lived. And when he found Adnah, he would take her as his own.

Yahweh, if You exist, protect my Adnah and keep her safe among the Assyrians.

SIX

"Again Abraham bowed down before the [Hittites] and he said to
Ephron in their hearing . . . 'I will pay the price of the field.
Accept it from me so I can bury my dead there.'
So the field and the cave in it were deeded to Abraham
by the Hittites as a burial site."
Genesis 23:12-13; 20

Two Weeks Later — Jotbah — Adnah

I ladled a second scoop of red stew into Haruz's wooden
bowl and placed it on the table before him. He lifted a
spoonful into his mouth and quirked one side of his
mouth. "Still not as good as Nenet's, but you're getting better."

Chuckling at my husband's awkward compliment, I ladled a
generous helping into my bowl. "Perhaps I should let you do
the cooking, and I'll fill the orders for scrolls."

"You're better at cooking than writing," he said as I sat on
the cushion beside him. "I'm quite good at writing, Adnah.
Why would anyone pay *you* to do it?"

I gave him a playful nudge and patted my rounded belly. "You write, and I'll take care of our baby."

All humor left his expression. He set down his spoon and pulled me close. "Nenet won't be here to help you, and what if—"

His cheek rested against my forehead, and I felt the quiver of emotion strangle his words. So many fears plagued me too. Nenet's death two years ago had been a turning point for us. We'd barely survived our first three winters in Jotbah, scraping together only enough supplies to carry us from small harvest to small harvest. When she lay dying of lung sickness, she whispered her long-held secret, directing me to the plain gold ring tucked in her belt—a forty-year-old betrothal promise from Master Joseph, never kept.

Devastated by his abba's detestable character, Haruz insisted we use the gold ring to purchase a proper burial location for Nenet. The Israelites in Jotbah refused, hating us because we were Judean—ancient tribal divisions ran deep. So Haruz purchased the field beside our home from a Hittite. "As Abraham purchased Hittite property to bury Sarah," he said with dignity, "so we will bury our ima and friend." Two months later—beside Nenet—we buried our stillborn child. The Hittite midwife witnessed Haruz's tender way with me, his incredible mind, and his writing skills on the lovely shard of pottery he gave her as a gift.

The next week, thanks to the midwife's kind referrals, Haruz was the busiest scribe within a day's journey.

"What if the Assyrians no longer need a scribe?" His voice was a whisper against my hair as if speaking it out loud would make it so.

I shook my head, refusing to answer. Most people from Jotbah had been taken away, their homes now occupied by strangers. People from other lands, speaking languages we didn't understand, were now wearing our friends' clothes and tending their gardens. "The soldiers stationed here need a scribe to communicate with their commanders," I said, hoping it was true. "We're safe here."

Footsteps outside our curtained doorway startled us. Haruz bolted to his feet, grabbed his walking stick, and stood by the door. I held my breath and waited for someone to appear. *Yahweh, protect us!*

A callused hand pulled aside our curtain, and a vaguely familiar face appeared. The man grabbed Haruz's stick and threw it to the floor. "You wouldn't know what to do with a weapon." He strode into our one-room home. "Your abba wants to know why you've stopped sending silver." He swayed as he spoke.

Ibri? Sudden recognition of our long-ago guide came with white-hot fury. "Joseph didn't deserve a single piece of that silver. Haruz sent it because he is a good and faithful son who—"

"Adnah." Haruz's stern tone silenced me. Extending his hand to the rude man, he motioned toward our small table. "We have stew. Sit. Eat."

"I've come for silver. Nothing else." Ibri reeked of stale wine. He'd probably drink away half the silver before returning to Jerusalem.

Haruz stepped toward the clay jar where we kept our valuables. "Adnah, please prepare a bag of bread and cheese for his journey while I gather what silver we can spare." The man watched his every move. Would he try to take more by force?

I moved to our food supplies, pulled a bag from the wall hook, and began filling the bag with the items Haruz mentioned. A shadow loomed over me, and suddenly our small room was filled with tumbling men. Pressing myself against the wall, I covered a scream and watched Haruz somehow overpower a man who had been nothing but hateful to us both.

Ibri lay splayed on his stomach, Haruz's knee pressed in his back and his head locked in my husband's arms. "You will not touch my wife." Haruz spoke in a terrifying low rumble.

"Moldy," the man choked out.

"What?" Haruz loosened his hold around Ibri's neck.

"I need moldy bread," he said more clearly, "so the Assyrian scouts won't steal it on my way back to Jerusalem."

Haruz's face paled, and he helped the man stand. "Forgive me," he said with a slight bow. "I thought you were . . ."

Ibri grabbed the pouch of silver from Haruz and a moldy loaf from our bucket of waste. "I underestimated you." The hint of a smile curved his lips as he pressed pieces of silver inside the moldy bread. "Your abba wouldn't believe you were anything but a weak imbecile, so I'll let him believe the silver comes from the girl's . . . talents."

"It's my talent." Haruz straightened, chest out. "I write contracts, betrothals, bills of sale—first for the Hittites, now for the Assyrians."

The man's brows rose. "You can write?"

Something in his tone sounded warning shofars in my mind. Would he try to take advantage of my kind-hearted husband as others had? "How did you make it this far north when the Assyrians have closed Israel's borders?" I asked, hoping to change the subject and protect my innocent husband from Joseph's henchman.

"Yes, I can write anything," Haruz answered, unwilling to be overlooked. He picked out a shard from our small pile of broken pottery and dipped his favorite reed in water to wet the black pigment. "What would you like me to write for you? Consider it a gift."

"My name," he said, eyes narrowing as he scowled at my husband. "Write my name: Ibri *ben Joseph*."

Haruz set the reed to the shard, forming the letters as he spoke them. "I-b-r-i b-e-n J-o—" He halted, lifting the reed but not lifting his eyes. "My abba's name is Joseph, and I'm Haruz ben Joseph. From which tribe and clan does your abba come, Ibri?"

I held my breath and prayed. *Yahweh, please . . . no.*

"The tribe of Levi. The clan of Abidan."

Haruz's hand began to shake as *Abidan*—Joseph's abba's name—hung in the air. He shifted from right foot to left. Right, left, right, left. The rocking grew more frantic, and I slipped my hand around his to help him finish the letters, *Ibri ben Joseph.* Ibri was Haruz's brother.

"Shall I ask him to leave?" I whispered.

Breathing unsteady, Haruz shook his head, eyes still averted, and continued rocking. Right then left, again and again, while Ibri stared at him with a sneer etched in granite.

Finally, Haruz laid aside the reed and clasped his hands. "My ima got sick when I was young. How did your ima die?"

The revelation of an illegitimate son raised many questions in both social and legal standing for the whole family, but the tender question Haruz asked widened Ibri's eyes and cracked his granite features. "I, uh . . . you would know better than me. You buried Nenet."

"Nenet was your ima?" A mixture of disbelief and disgust swelled in my belly, remembering how he'd ignored her five years ago while bringing us to Jotbah. "How could you—"

"The only person Nenet ever loved was Joseph." The stony glint returned to his eyes. "I was raised as a fatherless child, serving in Joseph's house during his first marriage. When I reached twelve, I joined the army and never looked back."

"Humph." Haruz pulled out a piece of clean of parchment and reached for his reed again. Without a word, he folded his legs and sat on a cushion, bent over his new writing project without a hint of its contents to me or his newly-introduced brother.

I glanced at the hardened soldier who suddenly looked as awkward as a schoolboy. Avoiding my gaze, he searched for another moldy loaf of bread and, upon finding it, stuffed the remaining pieces of silver inside and nestled three hunks of hard cheese into his riding pack.

"I won't trouble you further," he said, hurrying past me. "May the gods favor the child."

"Yahweh," I said.

"What?" He halted as if I'd speared him.

"Yahweh will bless this baby." I held his gaze and offered a smile. "We've trusted in only one God, and He hasn't failed us."

"You're not leaving." Haruz stood beside us now, holding out a scroll to his brother.

Ibri took it. "What's this?"

"A legal document declaring you the owner of the field next to our house." When Ibri's gaping mouth rendered him speechless, Haruz explained, "Adnah and I purchased the field where your ima is buried with the gold betrothal ring our abba gave her over forty years ago. That land should be yours—is yours—and we'd like to rent it from you for planting. You're welcome to stay here, in our loft, until you can build a home on the land."

Now, I was as shocked as my new brother-in-law. Haruz seemed befuddled by our amazement. "Family takes care of family," he said, drawing me to his side as he addressed Ibri. "It's why I send silver to Abba, and it's why you'll stay here with us until the Assyrians clear out of Israel and it's safe for you to travel back to Jerusalem."

Ibri blinked as if waking from a dream. He looked several times from me and then to Haruz. Back to me and to his brother again. And then a brilliant, wide smile lit the man's face. A low chuckle emerged as he shook his head. "You are no imbecile, Haruz, but you are indeed the strangest man I've ever known." He pressed his fist against his heart. "And I vow loyalty to you, my brother, for the rest of my days."

Haruz released me and wrapped Ibri in one of his big-bear

hugs. Though my heart wasn't as ready to embrace my new brother-in-law, I couldn't stop a grin. The man who had walked into our home an enemy would now stay in our home as family —because of my husband's ferocious love. It had softened Nenet's hardened heart and would salve years of Ibri's pain. How could I resist it? *Thank You, Yahweh, for giving me a husband who teaches me the deepest kind of love.*

PART III

ADNAH'S VENGEANCE —
THE FUTURE FORETOLD

Seven

"In the first month of the first year of [Hezekiah's] reign, he opened the doors of the temple of the Lord and repaired them. He brought in the priests and the Levites . . . and said: 'Listen to me, Levites! Consecrate yourselves now and consecrate the temple of the Lord . . . Remove all defilement from the sanctuary.'"
2 Chronicles 29:3-5

ca. 715 B.C. — Jerusalem — Shebna

"When we arrive at my abba's house," Shebna instructed Judah's royal guards, "you will treat him with respect but disregard his commands."

"Yes, my lord." The captain kept his focus forward, as did the ten guards marching behind them.

"Abba's mind has grown addled with age," Shebna explained. "He can be dangerous, so one guard must remain with me while the others gather the packed baskets from my chamber." He didn't dare confess that Abba was still strong as an ox and just as stubborn. Shebna feared he'd try to force his last faithful son to live at home.

"We are at your command, my lord," the captain said. "You will be moved into the palace by midday."

My lord. Moved into the palace. The words poured like warm honey into Shebna's ears. When King Ahaz had died a month ago, Judah's freedom to worship any god they chose died with him. Crown Prince Hezekiah was a devout Yahwist—and also Shebna's childhood classmate—so Shebna gladly embraced his Levite heritage when now *King* Hezekiah chose him to oversee renovations on Yahweh's temple. When halfway through the project Shebna proved his administrative acumen, the new king appointed him to the most influential position in court.

Shebna ben Joseph was now *palace administrator,* the one man in Judah who controlled access to the throne. No one—not even Queen Zibah—saw Hezi during court hours without Shebna's approval. Finally, he'd gained the power he'd so longed for and deserved.

"Get out of my house!" Abba shouted, as Shebna and the soldiers marched past him. "Who do you think you are?" His face grew crimson when the first soldier emerged with a packed basket from Shebna's room. "Thief! Put that back!"

Shebna approached him, perfectly calm. "Abba, they're taking *my* belongings to the palace. I'm on the king's council now and will reside in the palace administrator's chamber."

"You'll stay here as I command!" The blustering old fool grabbed Shebna's shoulders. "You're still my son."

Shebna laughed at the absurdity and shoved him aside. The captain reached out to catch him, but Abba fell hard over a low table, and let out a blood-curdling yowl. "My hip! My hip!"

The guard looked at Shebna, horrified and dumbstruck.

"Why didn't you catch him?" Shebna shouted.

"Why did you push him?" the big man replied.

"What did you say?" Shebna's seething challenge seemed to remind the guard of his station.

Straightening his spine and swallowing hard, the captain replied, "I should have caught your abba, my lord. A thousand apologies. May I fetch the king's physician?"

Shebna hid a grin with a nod, acknowledging the man's compliance. *Power.* It was intoxicating.

"Yes, bring the physician," Abba said before Shebna could answer.

"No! No need to bother the king's physician." Shebna glared at Abba while instructing the guard. "Abba's wife will take him to her family's farm in Bethlehem and tend him there." The old man would never bully Shebna again.

"No! Guard!" Abba cried. "See how he hates me? Don't let him take me from Jerusalem. My young wife is worthless."

"See what I mean?" Shebna tapped his head with one finger, reminding the captain of Abba's addled mind, and then glimpsed Naomi peeking around the kitchen doorway. "Come and tend your husband while I make sure the guards transfer everything I'll need." The girl, barely sixteen years old, dutifully attended Abba though he slapped her hands away each time she tried to touch him.

The captain, voice low, spoke for Shebna's ears alone. "Forgive me if I overstep, my lord, but my saba broke his hip when I was young. Even with the best physicians, he never recovered. I pray Yahweh takes your abba quickly—for both your sakes."

"Thank you, Captain." The man had no idea how long Shebna prayed that *any* god would kill his abba. When the guards had taken all his possessions out of Abba's home, Shebna instructed the captain to tell their king he'd be along shortly. "I'll make the arrangements for Abba and Naomi and return to the palace in time for the afternoon court proceedings." The captain saluted with his fist to his chest, and was gone.

When Shebna turned to check on Abba, he nearly toppled

over Naomi, who had silently crept up behind him. She was the only creature on earth frailer than he. "I could have hurt you!"

"Is he dying?" Was it hope or concern in her voice?

"I'll hire a cart to take you both to Bethlehem." He would ignore her question.

"What about a physician?" Abba whimpered. "All my sons have abandoned me. I can't afford a physician."

Shebna rolled his eyes, but what little Abba had saved might be given to Naomi or her family if they proved kind in Abba's last days. "You won't starve or go without a physician, Abba."

Shebna herded the wraith-of-a-woman toward a quiet corner to speak privately. Her eyes darted side to side like a frightened bird. "Naomi, as palace administrator, I now hold authority over the royal scribes. Since you've given Abba no children, a divorce will be simple."

"But a divorce will shame my family and—"

"They'll witness how badly Abba treats you," Shebna continued. "Although you have no legal claim to anything in Abba's household, I will pay you an allowance while you care for him." She wrung her hands, the shadow of uncertainty darkening the hollows beneath her eyes. He needed to sweeten the porridge. "A divorced woman is, of course, free to marry again when her ex-husband dies. I would consider it an honor to help facilitate a betrothal after an appropriate mourning period for Abba has been observed."

"I see you two conniving," Abba said between clenched teeth. "You'll get nothing, Shebna; not a single piece of my silver. I'll give it all to Haruz and Ibri."

"I'll do it," Naomi whispered. "How soon can we divorce?"

Shebna laughed and returned to stand over his abba. "I don't need your silver, old man, and I tire of your empty threats. The sons of your first wife disowned you. You don't even know where Haruz lives. And any judge would give *me* your estate over your favorite temple guard that absconded ten years ago."

"He's not just a guard," Abba snorted. "Ibri is your brother, and he's returning to Jerusalem."

Shebna steadied himself against the wall, while a thousand thoughts raced in dizzying circles through his mind. How could a shriveled old man still find ways to twist a knife in his belly? An illegitimate brother? How many others had Joseph ben Abidan abused? Shebna thought as palace administrator he'd climbed high enough to avoid Abba's barbs. But the old man's words weren't just barbs. They were *arrows*, sharp as obsidian and flung too hard to escape.

Shebna glared at his living curse, still lying on the floor. Abba stared back, defiant.

A delicate hand touched his shoulder and tugged. Shebna leaned down to hear Naomi whisper, "Take your revenge, Shebna," she said, voice shaky, "and add to it the vengeance of every woman Joseph has abused. I'll tend him at my family's farm only if he can't hurt me or anyone else I care about."

He straightened, his eyes finding hers, impressed by the hate he saw there, and in that moment something inside him shifted. "I swear by all the power of the gods, he'll never hurt anyone again." He was looking at Naomi but saw Adnah's face. He promised revenge for all, but only the hope of bringing Adnah back to Jerusalem could induce him to real vengeance.

Still lying on his side, Abba had never taken his eyes off Shebna. When his son knelt beside him, the old man asked nervously, "What are you doing?"

Shebna gently placed both hands on his hips. "Shh," he said tenderly. "Where does it hurt, Abba?"

"It hurts everywhere," he shouted. "Don't touch me!"

"As you wish." Leveraging himself on the old man's hips, Shebna abruptly pushed to his feet, and felt his abba's bones shift.

Joseph ben Abidan shrieked in agony, and deep satisfaction straightened Shebna's spine. "Goodbye, Abba," he shouted over lingering cries as he walked toward the door. "I'll instruct the guards at Jerusalem's gates to watch for Ibri's arrival. They'll make sure he tells us where Haruz and Adnah are, and I'll finally marry the woman you took away."

After fifteen years of waiting, Shebna had both the means and opportunity to find the only woman he'd ever loved, dissolve her marriage to Haruz, and marry her himself. Power was sweet—but vengeance was sweeter.

EIGHT

"Hezekiah sent word to all Israel and Judah...
inviting them to come to the temple of the Lord in Jerusalem
and celebrate the Passover to the Lord, the God of Israel...
When all this had ended, the Israelites who were there went out to
the towns of Judah, smashed the sacred stones and cut down the
Asherah poles. They destroyed the high places and the altars...
After they had destroyed all of them,
the Israelites returned to their own towns."
2 Chronicles 30:1; 31:1

Six Months Later — Adnah

My husband's rhythmic, wide sweeps with the cradle-scythe laid the ripened barley on its side, allowing me to follow close behind and bundle the stalks for drying. We'd cleared nearly half a field in two days—not nearly quick enough to harvest all the ripened grain on the new farm Shebna's silver had purchased for us.

"Adnah, look!" Haruz leaned on his scythe, pointing south. "It's Ibri! He came back—and there's someone with him!"

Needing a rest, I stood but didn't dare look, too afraid of who the second man might be. *Please, Lord, not Shebna.* When Ibri went to Jerusalem last winter—his first trip in ten years— he'd hoped to confront Joseph about his inheritance but was met with news of the man's move to Bethlehem and Shebna's promotion to palace administrator. He'd told Shebna I was pregnant, and brought congratulations in the form of enough silver to purchase land, several animals, enough barley seed for winter planting, and a four-room house on the edge of Jotbah. At least, that was the happy report Ibri gave while Haruz was in the room.

Later, when my husband left to deliver his contracts in Jotbah, Ibri explained the cuts and bruises on his face. Shebna used his new power and position to have Ibri beaten, demanding to know where we were and who had fathered my child. Ibri convinced him that Haruz was my baby's abba, but Shebna still refused to believe I loved my husband or that I was happy in Jotbah. With no little effort, Ibri convinced Shebna I wouldn't be willing to travel to Jerusalem to marry him, so Judah's palace administrator sent a scroll with Ibri—addressed to me alone:

To Adnah bat Perez,

From your eternally devoted brother, Shebna ben Joseph,

May you and your children's children find the happiness I've never had.

Instead of the anger I expected, Shebna hoped to bury me with guilt that wasn't mine to carry. I read his anger between the lines and spent the months since waiting. For what, I didn't know. The *Shebna* I'd known as a girl would never have ordered a man to be beaten. The *Shebna* I'd known as a girl was ambitious but kind, determined but honorable. But the palace administrator wanted revenge for the life Joseph—and Haruz— had stolen from him.

Would he come to Jotbah to make trouble?

Gathering my courage, I shaded my eyes and looked up at the two men approaching. The man with Ibri was equal in height and had shoulders like Haruz. Definitely not Shebna. Relief washed over me, and I arched my back to stretch tired muscles under the unrelenting summer sun.

The tell-tale ripping of my womb sent me to my knees.

Crying out, I cradled my over-sized belly. *Not again, Yahweh. Please. Not again.* Another contraction, this one more violent than the first, told me another of my children would meet Yahweh today.

Tears stung my eyes. I'd been working too much. This farm, Shebna's gift, was too much. Why didn't I tell Haruz I couldn't help? Why didn't I stop Ibri from returning to Jerusalem in the first place? He didn't need his rights as a son. We were happy in Jotbah, the three of us a family.

But two still-births and three miscarriages had robbed me of more than downy-soft babes at my breast. A broken heart had stolen my spirit. My joy. My very essence. I was an apparition.

"Adnah, are you—" Haruz knelt beside me, silenced by the blood running down my leg. He looked up at me, tears in his eyes. "I shouldn't have let you work the fields. You're too far along and—"

"We shouldn't have accepted it from Shebna. It's too big. We can't afford help."

He couldn't have looked more hurt if I'd slapped him. Nodding once, he scooped me into his arms and pulled me close. "I'm sorry, Adnah. It's my fault."

But it wasn't. I shook my head and buried my face in the curve of his neck, hating myself all the more. "It's not your fault." It was *me*. I'd lost five children *before* we accepted the farm from Shebna. I cried out with another contraction just as Ibri and the stranger approached.

Eyes wide, Ibri didn't even greet us. "I'll get the midwife!"

He dropped his travel bag and ran, leaving the stranger in the field alone.

Haruz placed me on our mule and swung himself on behind me, making the trek more bearable by cradling me close each time a contraction stole more hope. By the time we crossed our expansive property and reached our four-room house, Ibri was there with the midwife. The pity on her deeply-lined features was more than I could bear. I hid my face against Haruz's chest while he carried me to our bedchamber. He laid me on the straw-stuffed mattress. Even after months in this place, it felt like someone else owned it, like strangers would return and demand that we leave.

Another contraction ripped through me. I fisted the bed covers. Let out a shriek but silently begged. *Why, Yahweh? Why take another?* Panting in the silence, I felt a cool cloth on my head and the midwife's breath on my cheek. "We'll get through this one too, my friend."

She patted my leg and shooed Haruz out. "I'll take good care of her and give her poppy-seed tea after. I'll call you when we're finished, but she'll likely sleep through the night."

When we're finished. It sounded so simple. Losing a life. Changing a future. Letting go of dreams.

Another contraction, and the midwife took her place behind me. Lifting my shoulders, she whispered softly against my ear, "Lean into the pain, my friend. The sooner it's over . . . the sooner it's over."

***

I woke, blanketed by my husband's arms and legs while his whole body shook. My hair, shoulder, and sheep's-wool head-rest were wet with his tears. I could never love anyone the way I adored this gentle giant-of-a-man. Stroking his dark, curly hair, I tried to soothe him. "Haruz, my love, I am well."

He sniffed and wiped his face on his sleeve, raising his head to look into my eyes. "I asked you to work the field, and working caused us to lose our child."

"No!" His guilt pierced me. "It wasn't your fault. Or Shebna's for giving us the land. I simply can't deliver a healthy baby." Despair welled up within me, and I pulled away, turning on my side to face the wall. "I can't give you a child, Haruz. The Law says you should marry another."

He tugged my shoulder, turning me to face his furrowed brow. "The Law *allows* me to marry another, but I love you, Adnah. Only you—ever." His eyes filled with tears again. "Ibri brought a hired hand and . . . news."

It wasn't like my husband to be coy. He was neither capable of lying, nor able to keep a secret. "Tell me," I said, bracing myself for the worst.

"Abba is dead. Remember, when Ibri returned from his first trip, he said Abba had fallen months before?" I nodded. "Ibri said Abba never recovered, and instead of burying him in our family cave, Shebna buried him in the pauper's field outside Jerusalem." Haruz's brows dipped in confusion. "Why would Shebna do that?"

Remembering that Shebna had beaten Ibri mercilessly, I had my suspicions about Joseph's injuries as well as his burial. "It's been many years since we've left Jerusalem. Perhaps the Shebna we once knew isn't the same man who now serves as palace administrator."

Haruz looked as if I'd thrown a cup of cold water in his face. "What if he didn't make proper sacrifices for Abba before he died? I know we'll see our children in Paradise, Adnah, but is my abba in Sheol?" His final words were muffled on my sleeve, pouring out more tears for an abba who didn't deserve them.

I placed my hand atop his head with what little strength I had, pondering the actions of the other brother I once thought I loved. If Shebna could buy us land, animals, and a home, he could certainly afford to bury Joseph properly. But he *chose* vengeance. I might have done the same. Haruz's merciful tears condemned me. Never would it cross my husband's mind to mete out justice for his abba's abuse. For Haruz, right was right, and doing wrong was unthinkable. For Shebna, had all these years with Joseph turned him into—the unthinkable?

"Let me write to him."

Startled from his grief, he looked up, a deep crease between his brows. "What would you say?"

"I would thank him for undertaking the burial details and ask if proper sacrifices were made." I watched a war rage behind his eyes. "Perhaps it would ease your mind," I added.

"Or confirm my fears." He bowed his head with a deep sigh.

I waited silently, giving my husband time to think. The oil lamp sputtered in the wall niche. A cock crowed at dawn's light. I closed my eyes, considering what I'd write in my first letter to the man I'd planned to marry fifteen years ago—half a lifetime.

"Ibri also brought news." I opened my eyes and found my husband's gaze on me. "The new king, Hezekiah, has invited faithful Yahweh worshipers from Israel to celebrate Passover in Jerusalem." He reached up to push some hair off my forehead. "I'll take you back to Shebna now. I never intended to hold you captive or hurt you."

"You think I—"

"Shebna can give you nice things, Adnah. Maybe he can make you smile again. Become *you* again."

I covered a sob, shaking my head. His words felt like a dagger in my belly while years of sadness heaped onto my back like great boulders. I'd walked in the shadows so long, my beloved believed *he* was the cause. *Yahweh, forgive me.*

Finding strength, I pulled him into a ferocious hug and whispered through tears. "I'm not going to Jerusalem, Haruz ben Joseph. Your love neither holds me captive nor hurts me. On the contrary, it is your love that frees and strengthens me." I kissed him on his cheeks, his eyes, his forehead, and finally on his mouth—lingering there, desperate for him to know how I adored him. Enveloped in his massive frame, I let the steady beating of his heart soothe me. "We'll write a letter to Shebna together."

He squeezed me tighter. "We'll write it, and I'll hand it to him when I celebrate my first Passover."

"No!" I tried to pull away, but he held me in his embrace.

"I must see him, Adnah. I must know if my brother . . . is still my brother."

Though terror shot through me at the thought of Haruz's return to Jerusalem, something deeper inside wanted Shebna to encounter my competent, successful husband. I wanted Judah's palace administrator to know I'd fallen in love with the better brother.

***

Joshua, the hired hand Ibri brought from Jerusalem, worked with the other two men of my household from dawn 'til dusk, and within two weeks all our barley was harvested. Ibri volunteered to stay with me, refusing to see Shebna—ever again. "He's become a miniature version of Joseph," he said, confirming my fears. Haruz made excuses for Shebna, refusing to believe the worst of his favorite brother. He and Joshua joined a caravan bound for Jerusalem, carrying with them the first fruits of our crops.

Ibri spent his days preparing the fields for spring planting. I alternated cooking, laundry, and resting, still weary from losing our sixth child. But something inside me had shifted after Haruz had grieved his abba's death so deeply. His absolute certainty of seeing our children—and the uncertainty of his abba's fate—somehow freed me from my chains of sadness. During the month of Haruz's absence, instead of wishing I could hold my baby now, I imagined seeing all my children's faces in Paradise!

"You're humming." Ibri stood at the threshold of our door, a coy smile on his craggy face. "I haven't heard you sing for years."

I ducked my head, unaware of my humming but not surprised. It was proof that my joy had returned. Adding another cup of grain to the hand mill in my lap, I asked my friend, "Why aren't Haruz and Joshua back from Jerusalem? Passover and the Feast of Unleavened Bread only lasts seven days and they've been gone almost a month."

"Because King Hezekiah extended the celebration." My husband's voice snatched my attention, and I squealed, leaping off my stool and nearly toppling the hand mill to the floor. Quickly settling it on the floor, I ran to greet him. "You're back!" I flung my arms around his neck, and he squeezed me so tight I could barely breathe. I noticed Joshua standing beside Ibri—and a young woman stood a pace behind them both, head bowed and trembling. "Who—?"

"She's a gift from Shebna," my husband said, setting my feet on the floor.

A gift? My stomach clenched. Had Shebna given his brother a second wife to bear him sons? Was this my ex-suitor's revenge?

Before I could choose between anger or hurt, Haruz grabbed my arm and led me to the low table where we ate our meals. Pulling me down on a cushion beside him, he kept his voice at a whisper. "The Law says we're to stone idolaters, Adnah, but Shebna wanted me to bring her home—to you."

"To me?"

"As your handmaid." He tucked his head like a beaten dog. "When I told him you lost the baby, he said it was my fault for making you work the fields."

"Haruz, that's not true."

"She can work the fields for you," he said, ignoring me, "but also lighten your household chores. Shebna insisted I take her even though she was a priestess at one of the pagan shrines in Jerusalem."

I covered a gasp and looked at the girl, my stomach twisting into knots. *Shebna insisted.* She was to be his revenge for my refusal to leave Haruz. Shebna sent a beautiful priestess to steal my husband's heart from Yahweh and from me. A woman to bear him children. Her trembling didn't seem so pitiful now. Women like her were the reason I was sold to pay my abba's debts.

"After Passover," Haruz continued, "some Israelites in our caravan—zealous for Yahweh—began destroying pagan high places and cutting down Asherah poles. Shebna and some of the king's guards caught up with us and brought Talitha. They said she was one of their *favorites.* I've made it clear she will worship Yahweh only—or die." Looking over his shoulder, Haruz scowled at the girl.

"Haruz," I said, touching his arm gently, hoping to soothe the formidable stranger before me. I'd never seen him so riled or heard him threaten death even when the Assyrians terrorized us. I looked beyond him at young Joshua, who spoke quietly with Ibri, eyes wide and hands moving in dramatic gestures. Something significant happened in Jerusalem—more than Haruz was telling. I brushed my husband's cheek. "What happened when you went to the palace to speak with Shebna?"

"Shebna doesn't follow Yahweh, Adnah, and he lies to the king. He's mean and angry now. I don't ever wish to return to Jerusalem, and I don't wish to speak of it. If the girl worships an idol, she dies. If she disobeys you, she goes. I owe nothing more to Shebna."

The girl, Talitha, stood five paces from us. Alone. Separate. Chin raised, pallor gray, she was the picture of terrified strength. Her whole world had turned upside down, and she had no idea that the God of all Creation had chosen to save her through this terrifying man named Haruz.

I grasped both sides of his bushy beard and drew him close, forcing him to look into my eyes. "You won Nenet and Ibri with your love, Husband. What makes you think Talitha requires a different approach?" He tried to look away, but I held him fast. "I don't know what happened between you and Shebna, but that girl isn't responsible for your brother's poor choices. We will repay Shebna's vengeance by showing his priestess Yahweh's mercy and kindness."

A spark of anger flared in his eyes before his gentle spirit doused it. "Uhh-ull right," he grunted. Standing, he faced our growing family. "Talitha!" The girl stiffened, her face growing paler. "You may choose a robe from my wife's clothing as our gift to you. Ibri, show Joshua and me what you've accomplished in our absence." He started toward the door, and Talitha stepped out of the way, giving all three men wide berth as they left for the fields.

She watched them all the way to the edge of the nearest field and then turned to me. "You must teach me how to control a man so completely," she said. "He was a caged bear until he saw your face, and then he was clay in your hands."

Working hard not to be offended, I patted the cushion beside me. She moved it an arm's-length from me and knelt, still cautious. "Love doesn't control," I said, "and you'll realize Haruz is a good and kind master."

"My last 'good and kind master' waited a whole week before taking me to his bed." She surveyed our gathering area, tilted her head, and looked at me with a smirk. "You have no children. I'd say *this* good and kind master will take me within three days if I choose the right robe. Which way to your bedchamber?" She stood and waited.

Speechless, I felt the blood drain from my face and couldn't make my legs move. In the silence, the insolent young woman's armor began to crack. Subtle quaking in her chin followed by a sheen of tears soon gave way to defiant sniffing.

I rose to my feet, reached for her hand, and held her gaze. "I was sold as a servant to Haruz's abba to pay my family's debts. How did you become a priestess, Talitha?"

Surprise restored some color to her cheeks. "My abba died, fighting the Philistines in Prince—I mean, *King* Hezekiah's regiment. I have six brothers and sisters. Ima is sick and can't work, so I—" Bowing her head, she swiped at her eyes. When she looked up again, her cheeks were rosy, and her eyes were dry. "Lord Shebna and others like him were very good to me and my family."

"No, love. They weren't." My heart ached at the lies she'd believed. "They trapped you in a life with no escape—but Yahweh found a way to rescue you." I drew her into a hug and felt her relax in my embrace. Shebna had fallen into his own trap. My vengeance would become Yahweh's lovingkindness shown to the girl he'd hoped would wreak havoc in our home. *Thank You, Yahweh, for bringing Talitha into our strange little family. Help us love her well.*

NINE

"This is what the Lord, the Lord Almighty, says [to Isaiah the prophet]: 'Go, say to this steward, to Shebna the palace administrator: What are you doing here and who gave you permission to cut out a grave for yourself . . . Beware, the Lord is about to take firm hold of you and hurl you away, you mighty man."
Isaiah 22:15-17

Three Years Later — Jerusalem — Shebna

Shebna stood in the courtyard of a small, dilapidated house on the far west side of Upper Jerusalem where he watched a palace servant deliver the last basket of his belongings, turn around, and leave. Alone. Shebna was alone. City sounds filled the air—children playing, women chatting, angry men. None of them knew Isaiah and Eliakim ruined his life today. No one cared that he'd worked harder than anyone. Was smarter than everyone. Had wielded more power than all but one—the king.

Until Isaiah turned Hezi against him.

When Shebna returned from Egypt four weeks ago, Hezi had lauded his diplomatic success. The gods of the Black Land had answered Shebna's secret prayers by coaxing Pharaoh So to sign a treaty in which both nations refused to pay tribute to Assyria. The Egyptian-Judean Coalition would strengthen military and trade relations between their nations and had certainly strengthened Shebna's standing with Judah's king. Hezi was so pleased, he'd given his palace administrator a generous percentage of the treasure he'd brought home from Egypt— which Shebna had immediately used to begin construction on his burial cave. A cave that rivaled Pharaoh So's in luxury and would honor the Egyptian gods who had blessed Shebna's work.

Only a few weeks into the construction, Isaiah barged into a court proceeding and prophesied Yahweh's wrath on Shebna, turning Hezekiah and most of his royal counsel against him. The king stripped Shebna of all authority, lands, and wealth gained as palace administrator, demoted him to a paltry royal secretary, and made his best friend Eliakim the new palace administrator. Since Shebna, a Levite, had no family property, the king gifted a small house to him in the Upper City.

"For your years of faithful service," he'd said. Hezi's pity only added to the humiliation.

Shebna's bitterness bloomed into hatred when he received a message written in Haruz's own hand:

To Shebna, my brother, in your time of trouble.

When King Hezekiah's guards came to seize the house, animals, and farm, they gave no reason—saying only that your property now belonged to Judah's king.

I write this as an offering of gratitude for your years of provision and to assure you that we find no hardship in giving it up. Ibri never sold his plot of land or his cottage, so Adnah and I have returned there to live with him. He is quite ill, and we hope Adnah's herbal skills can revive his health.

*Talitha served Adnah as both maid and friend. We cancelled
her debt, and she married our farmhand, Joshua. Since we had no
room for them in the cottage, they have returned to Judah in hopes
of starting a new life.*

*If Jerusalem has become too hard to bear, Shebna, join our
family in Jotbah. Farm life is simple but rewarding. Yahweh will
bless you here as He has blessed us.*

From your devoted brother, Haruz ben Joseph

Shebna crushed the parchment and rolled it into a ball. *Join
their family in Jotbah?* Did Haruz think he could be satisfied
scratching in dirt? Shebna had counseled kings! Must Adnah
return to the fields again? White-hot rage burned in his belly,
churning and roiling like a stormy sea. He released a guttural
roar at the sky, shaking with rage, then fell to his knees and
retched in a discarded clay pot.

Wiping the vomit from his beard, he stood and straightened
the only robe he owned. He must regain control. Of his life. His
dignity. For years, he'd sent letters with gifts to Adnah, making
sure she knew every accomplishment, every success—hoping
she'd leave Haruz, the dim-witted brother, and return to the
one who could give her the life she deserved. He scanned the
disheveled courtyard, the broken wooden shutters on the
windows, and the overgrown myrtle tree. With a little work, he
could make it a modest but respectable home.

"And when I have vengeance on Isaiah the prophet, Adnah
will wish she'd chosen me."

***

A Year Later

Shebna heard snoring in the foggy half-consciousness of
dawn's light. The woman sleeping beside him had been a gift.
She'd never be any man's slave. She wasn't his servant exactly.

Definitely not a wife. Belit was Babylon's chief sorceress. She had accompanied her master, Merodach-Baladan, the displaced king who came to pay homage to Hezekiah after his miraculous healing.

It all began with another of Isaiah's disastrous prophecies. Hezi grew deathly ill from a flea bite. Isaiah and his God condemned Hezi to death—largely because of the treaty he'd signed with Egypt years ago. It would seem Yahweh held a grudge as tightly as Shebna. But He showed a measure of mercy when Isaiah changed his prophecy, saying He would give Hezekiah fifteen years before He killed him.

All this happened while 180,000 Assyrians camped outside Jerusalem's gates, preparing for a siege. On the morning Hezi woke completely healed, the 180,000 Assyrians didn't wake at all. Isaiah used the timely coincidence to persuade Hezi it was another of Yahweh's miracles. Anyone with a shred of sense could see the flea-infested Assyrians died from the same illness that nearly claimed the king.

The stories grew and spread through the trade routes. Shebna and the other royal secretaries could hardly keep pace, recording all the tribute and gifts from visiting dignitaries who came to glimpse the divinely-touched king that sent the other half of Assyria's army scampering back to Nineveh.

No one was more interested in conquering the Assyrians than the Babylonian rebel, Merodach-Baladan. Since Shebna had cultivated a diplomatic relationship with him on a previous journey to Babylon, Hezi had summoned Shebna yesterday to show Merodach the great wealth of Judah's kingdom.

"You, little man, are to be my master," Belit said to Shebna as he finished the tour.

Panicked, he turned to Merodach, prepared to apologize—though he'd done nothing wrong.

Rather than the indignation he expected, Shebna watched a knowing grin curve the displaced king's lips as he turned toward his sorceress. "I've learned never to argue with her, Shebna, so she is yours—if you will use her skills to destroy the Assyrians."

Of course, Shebna accepted her as a gift and agreed to Merodach's terms. But if Belit truly had power to destroy, he would aim it at someone closer than Assyria. Isaiah would learn there were many gods more powerful than the antiquated Yahweh he and Hezekiah insisted Judah must worship.

Rising up on one elbow, Shebna hovered over the sleeping sorceress, studying her. She was a giant, as tall as any royal guard with shoulders to match. Her features were plain but not ugly. Black, straight hair lay across her face, and one arm rested over her head.

Suddenly, her eyes shot open, and like black beads, they looked through him. "Your Adnah is dead, but the child lives."

A cold sweat overtook Shebna, but he couldn't look away. He hadn't even known Adnah was pregnant. Was this a trick? Had someone paid this woman to torment him? "How do you know her name?"

Belit sat up, her muscular frame towering over his weakness. "The child can help us."

Like hornets, thoughts buzzed in his head followed by a sudden, piercing pain. "Stop! Stop this!" He clutched at his thinning hair, but as quickly as it came, the pain left. He leapt out of bed, panting. "What did you do?"

Belit sat calmly, a mischievous smile taunting. "You are small, but you need not be weak, Shebna. I can teach you about my starry hosts."

"I have already studied your gods, Belit." Her presumption infuriated him. "I invite you to worship them in this house—as long as the king never learns of it."

Sliding off the bed, she approached him like a lioness on the hunt. She trapped his head between her mammoth hands and pressed her lips against his ear. "I've come to free you from the man you are and show you the prince you can become." The warmth of her breath made him forget everything except her voice. "You will be mighty, Shebna, if you release your past and embrace me—the seedbed of your future." She gripped his hands and placed them around her waist, pressing her body against his.

Thus began two days of worship.

Shebna's personal priestess mapped out their future while honoring the starry hosts that she served. They ate little, hardly slept, and never left his house. His chamber became the center of their world and the dawn of Shebna's new life. Mid-morning of the third day, a messenger called out from the courtyard gate. Shebna flung his robe around his shoulders and strode outside. The messenger held out a scroll.

Haruz's wax seal was covered with dust proving the long journey from Jotbah. Shebna paid the messenger and reached for the scroll, knowing its contents without breaking the seal. "Wait!" He stopped the messenger who looked about ten years old. "Is your master returning to Jotbah soon?" He was Haruz's age when Adnah first came to serve in Abba's household.

"My master said we'll gather supplies in Jerusalem and return to Jotbah by week's end."

"I've got a package I want you to deliver to the man who sent this message." He hurried into the house, directly to a clay cup on his kitchen shelf, and dumped the few pieces of silver he'd been saving into a small pouch. Then he walked to his study, removed a blank parchment from a stack, and scribbled these words:

From Shebna ben Joseph, Royal Secretary to King Hezekiah of Judah:

I have no desire to see a child that should have been mine. The enclosed silver should pay for a wet nurse. Each year I will send more silver to provide for crops that will feed the child. That much I must do for Adnah. I no longer have a brother.

He sensed Belit's presence behind him and then felt her

hands slip around his waist. He stood, and she placed her chin atop his head while he read the missive aloud. She chuckled and stepped toward the table, picking up the unopened scroll from Haruz, her eyes alight with jest. "You didn't even open—"

"I need no distractions from our plans, Belit. You already told me Adnah was dead, the child alive." He wrapped his note around his pouch of silver and placed the bundle in a secure leather sheath. "You've shown me the best way to honor Adnah's legacy is to avenge the wrongs committed against our love."

"How does giving away your silver avenge anything?" She reached for the leather pouch, but he pulled it away and started toward the door.

"Adnah was the only good thing the gods ever gave me," he said, pausing at the threshold to look back at the woman who would help him destroy Isaiah. "Until you arrived. Everything we do from this moment on, I'll consider *Adnah's vengeance.*"

Author's Note

Shebna is a biblical character, which means he was a real human being who lived and breathed and made a historical impact on God's people—an impact God wanted preserved in His eternal Word. Shebna is mentioned in nine Scripture passages (2 Kings 18:18, 26, 37; 19:2; Isaiah 22:15; 36:3, 11, 22; 37:2). He is described as King Hezekiah's palace administrator whose sin and pride gets him demoted to the position of secretary.

> "[The Lord said to Shebna through Isaiah,] 'I will depose you from your office . . . I will summon my servant, Eliakim son of Hilkiah. I will clothe him with your robe and . . . hand your authority over to him.'"
> **Isaiah 22:19-21**

Isaiah's Legacy tells the incredibly sad story of King Hezekiah's only son, King Manasseh. Hezekiah, the most righteous king of Judah, died exactly when the prophet Isaiah foretold, placing Manasseh on Judah's throne at the young age of twelve. Barely a man—even by ancient Middle Eastern standards—

Manasseh became Judah's wickedest king, a leader compared not only to other evil kings but also to the despicable Canaanites that Yahweh purged from the land.

> "But Manasseh led Judah and the people of
> Jerusalem astray, so that they did more evil
> than the nations the LORD had destroyed
> before the Israelites." ***2 Chronicles 33:9***

So, the purpose of the prequel, *Adnah's Legacy*, was to assure you that Shebna once had a heart. He learned to care for his brother deeply, someone with symptoms very similar to people you might know that have been diagnosed with Asperger's. Shebna also knew how to love but became the vilest villain I've ever written when his heart was destroyed by so much pain and betrayal. Let the heartless villain of *Isaiah's Legacy* be a real person before he's an enemy.

OF HEROES & KINGS

Prequel to Of Fire and Lions

PART I

NEBUDCHADNEZZAR –
MY POWER, MY WORLD

ONE

"Like a gold ring in a pig's snout is a beautiful woman who shows no discretion."
Proverbs 11:22

618 B.C. Simanu (June) — Achmetha, Median Empire — Amyitis

The unseasonably cool mountain air stiffened my fingers, making it impossible to fasten my sword belt over the blue linen gown. "Uhh! Mandane, help me tie this knot."

My younger sister's nimble hands finished the task, and she appraised me with a mischievous smirk. "Should I fetch your bow and quiver, sister? It would complement the sapphire necklace Mother left you."

With nerves stretched tight, I tried to decide if I should hate her or hug her. Her giggle snapped the tension, and I chose the hug. "Father should leave the dressing up to you and the fighting to me."

She squeezed me tighter. "You are *Princess Amyitis,* and you are more beautiful than you know."

I kissed her cheek and pulled away, hurrying toward the hand-held mirror on my bedside table. Maybe I could change my reflection into something more resembling Mandy's opinion of me.

"I'm sure Father summoned you this morning to tell you of a match," she said.

I stared into the polished-bronze, assessing my straight, brown hair and wide-set dark eyes. "Surely, Father has given up on my betrothal by now, Mandy."

She rested her chin on my shoulder, her loveliness reflected beside my plain features in the hand mirror. "You weren't trying to humiliate the Elamite prince or the Persian nobleman's son."

Again mischief sparkled in her eyes, but this time I was quite serious. "I refuse to marry a man I can best with a sword." My belly felt as if I'd swallowed a hornet's nest, like it did every time I thought of marrying. I slammed the mirror onto the table and reached for a simple leather string to tie my hair back at the nape of my neck.

Mandy whirled me to face her. "Amy, at least promise me if you meet another suitor this morning you'll wait until tomorrow to draw your sword." She wiggled her eyebrows and the hornets in my belly stopped their stinging.

"If I make such a promise, perhaps I should wear my bow." Our laughter was cut short by a loud rap on the door. "Coming!" I shouted and then whirled in a circle. "How do I look?"

Mandy's eyes traveled from my loosely-bound hair to my unshod feet. "A princess should wear shoes." She kicked off her sandals as our door swung open.

"Amy, you know your grandfather doesn't like to be kept wai--" He fell silent while watching me wriggle into Mandy's shoes, and a bright smile overshadowed his sternness at the sight of my sword. "I see you're ready to discuss another betrothal."

My father was a brilliant man, a powerful warrior, and a loyal co-ruler with my grandfather. But he was a magnificent father, who had raised Mandy and me with tenderness and care since our mother died from lung sickness five years before. He offered his right arm and escorted me out of the chamber.

"Be nice!" Mandy shouted as Father closed the door behind us.

"Your sister offers wise advice, my girl." He smiled, but the corners of his mouth twitched, betraying something hidden. We walked in silence on worn carpets that covered stone floors surrounded by stone walls in a city surrounded by mountains with jagged cliffs and punishing weather. The stark interior of our palace was the symbol of a Medes' life. Simple. Relentless. Focused.

"Mandy will be happy with any man her kings choose for her." Father's voice was gentle but firm. "Your grandfather and I will chose a kind and wealthy man for her next year, but likely a nobleman not royalty."

I wanted to ask why not royalty. Mandy was far more beautiful than I. She could spin and weave and cook better than many of the royal and noble women in Achmetha.

"But you, Amy..." He still hadn't looked at me. "You are more difficult."

We turned down the breezeway connecting the residence wing to the palace proper. Tall, slender windows allowed the mid-morning sun to warm the stone enclosure, but my father's comment sent a chill through me. *You are more difficult.* I turned the words over in my mind while my sword clanged against my thigh. Could my passion for the sword be what made me more difficult than Mandy? Father had placed a sword in my hand before Mother put shoes on my feet. Which, perhaps explained my aversion to shoes. But sword play was the one thing that defined me. It was the only thing I was really *good* at.

We'd entered the bustling corridor outside the Medes' high court, and my angst spilled into whispered hysteria. "Father, I don't want to be difficult, but please don't make me give up the sword. I know I'll never fight with the army, and I could let some of the new recruits best me in sword drills if that would help, but--"

He pulled me aside to a private corner, away from curious ambassadors and snickering Medes. I saw only love in his eyes. "You are difficult, my precious girl, because you are a rare jewel that I refuse to place in anything less than gold." He brushed my cheek with the back of his hand. "You are difficult *to match* because I have yet to meet a man worthy of you. Today, however, I believe we'll arrange for you to meet your match."

He kissed my forehead and wrapped my arm around his, resuming our march toward the twin-throned courtroom he and Grandfather had shared for nearly five years.

My panic grew with each step.

Dare I tell him the truth? I hadn't even told Mandy. I'd never even said the words aloud. Was it better to tell Father now--before I faced Grandfather Cyaxares? I'd always been able to share my heart with Father, but the other Median king had little patience for women--and even less for his grand-daughters. I took a deep breath and pulled him aside again, this time right beside the throne room doors.

"What is it?" Brows pulled together, his patience was thinning. "We've already kept your Grandfather waiting too--"

"I don't think I want to get married."

To his credit, his eyes bulged only momentarily before looking around us to be sure no one overheard. Straightening his already perfectly fitted robe, he offered his right arm again. "You will not refuse this betrothal, Amy."

I stared at his proffered arm. Studied the pinched creases between his nose and the hard set of his jaw. He was a Mede. A king. And I, the firstborn daughter of the most relentless warrior on earth. Straightening my spine, head held high, I laid my hand on his forearm and entered the courtroom to face the other king of the Medes.

Grandfather Cyaxares sat on the larger of two thrones made of marbled granite. Head bowed, reading a scroll, he was startled when his herald announced our arrival. "Our great co-regent and good King Astyages approaches with the pure and lovely Princess Amyitis."

The crowded room quieted to a curious hum. Grandfather scowled at us before leaning forward to address a contingent of five noblemen, who waited at the foot of his dais. The visitors turned in unison to appraise me as I assessed them. Their oiled and curled beards could have deemed them Assyrian or Babylonian, but robes and jewelry bearing the image of the mythical creature, Sirrush, identified their loyalty to the Babylonian god, Marduk. All five were older than Father, fatter than oxen, and leering at me like jackals.

Please, merciful Mithra, look upon your faithful daughter, and strike me dead if one of these men is to be my betrothed.

Father escorted me past the Babylonians, up the dais, and to a stool placed on the right of a granite throne only slightly smaller than Grandfather's. When Father sat down, Grandfather leaned over, whispering behind his hand. "You indulge her too much, Astyages." He turned his red face at me. "The next time you make me wait, young woman, I'll send my guards to fetch you--in *shackles*." He hissed the last word through gritted teeth, and I knew he meant it.

Father stood, ceasing his co-ruler's rant. "My esteemed friends from Babylon, I introduce to you my firstborn daughter, Amyitis, the joy of my life and crowning jewel of Media. As you see by the fire in her eyes and the sword at her waist, she is as fierce as she is lovely. A Median woman is like no other."

I felt like a mare in a market.

"Babylon cares more about the ferocity of your troops than

the fire of your women," said one Babylonian who wore more jewelry than my mother ever owned.

Father's hand rested on the hilt of his sword, and I hoped he would take off the man's head for such impertinence. Instead, he narrowed his eyes and crouched low, calling the man to climb two steps of the dais. The Babylonian, suddenly not so eager to be spokesman, nudged another man forward, but his friends refused. Finally, he climbed the steps and leaned close while Father whispered something in his ear that no one else could hear. The man's face grew paler while listening and he offered a single nod before returning to the other four ambassadors.

Father drew his dagger, the sing of its blade against the metal sheath wresting the Babylonian's attention. Every sound in the courtroom still, while King Astyages descended the steps and paused before the five envoys. Gripping the blade in his left hand, his right hand pulled down swiftly, sending a stream of fresh blood from his fist. Unflinching, he drizzled it over the envoys' heads while making his oath. "By the blood of a Mede and the hearts of its kings, the armies of Media and her surrounding tribal neighbors will join troops with King Nabopolassar of Babylon to destroy Assyria's empire by decimating the city of Nineveh."

He paused in front of the ambassador who had dishonored him moments earlier. "You will hold out their hands and take your vows in blood."

"But we've delivered King Nabopolassar's signed treaty," the man said, his eyes as round as the ruby pendant around his neck.

"Parchment means nothing to a Mede." Even though I saw only Father's back, I heard the delight in voice. He and Grandfather signed scroll treaties regularly, but he was making a point with these arrogant fools.

Slowly, each of the five men held out one trembling hand to

my father. He looked over their heads to make his final declaration to the Medes in our court. "In return for any Median lives lost in battle, King Nabopolassar vows to offer not only Babylon's troops but also every mercenary army under his command to restore Median rule to the city of Susa." Applause exploded, and every Mede in the room lifted his sword, answering their king's call to arms. My father shouted his final declaration over the hysteria. "And as a pledge of Babylon's and Media's lasting loyalty and kinship, this day we seal the betrothal of Babylon's crown prince and Media's Princess Amyitis."

With the speed and stealth of the Medes' fiercest warrior, Father nicked the hand of every Babylonian envoy before they realized they were bleeding. The arrogant, bejeweled man saw his blood dripping and fainted dead away. The others fisted their hands and tried to join the celebration.

I could barely breathe at the memory of Father's words. *You will not refuse this betrothal, Amy.*

This treaty could mean the end of Assyria's oppression and a more powerful Median kingdom. Some of the men would give their lives for Media's freedom. No, they would die for freedom. If only I could die with my sword for freedom--instead of live as a princess in Babylon.

TWO

Babylon — 1 Month Later

My head pounded. My legs ached. My stomach growled. And I'd spent too many nights sleeping in a tent on a reed mat to remember what a wool-stuffed mattress felt like. On this, our twentieth day atop a camel, Mandy and I sat on dusty pillows in our canopied sedan —baking in the Babylonian sun.

"How much farther?" Mandy's voice was a gravelly croak.

I emptied our waterskin onto a rag and pressed it against her dry, cracked lips. "Suck on this."

She nodded and obeyed, making me hate my betrothed even more. If he didn't live in this gods-forsaken desert, my sister wouldn't be suffering from heat fever. She could be spinning and weaving with the councilmen's wives and daughters, and I could be training with our troops. Not that I'd be joining them to fight in battles, but Father said I was quicker with a sword than most boys my age and proved valuable at sparring.

I wiped the sweaty tendrils from Mandy's brow and pressed the cloth against her forehead. The sun was past midday but even hotter than yesterday. Her head lolled back on a pillow; her eyes closed. She'd always been fragile—like Mother. The thought terrified me. I couldn't lose her. Even the thought of living in Babylon—being separated by ten to twenty days of travel, depending on the season—was more than I could bear.

Her eyes fluttered opened, and I turned away quickly, determined to hide traitorous tears.

"Stop it." She struggled to sit up and then tugged at my shoulder to make me face her. "You're marrying the future king of Babylon. Stop moping like you've been sentenced to death."

"It's not *my* death that concerns me," I said, frustration boiling over. "What if you or Father become ill? By the time a messenger could ride to Babylon and escort me back to Achmetha, nearly a month would pass. If I marry this *Nebuchadnezzar*, every time you and I say goodbye could be our last."

Her cheeks were still as red as fire, but her eyes softened to the sweet sister who always spoke to my heart. "Every time we say goodbye..." She reached for my hand, linking our little fingers as we always did to seal a vow. "Is another chance to make and keep a promise."

Our eyes locked, and my vow came first. "I will always come back, Mandy."

"And I promise no man will never come between us." Bold vows made by women in a man's world, but there was strength in my frail sister's countenance. Nothing—and no one—could divide our hearts.

"Babylon on the horizon!" The caravan master shouted over his shoulder, and a unified shout rose from the thousands of voices surrounding our royal party. Median troops marched boldly toward Babylon without fear or hesitation, while I suddenly fell trembling into the arms of my twelve-year-old sister.

Terror gripped me. I wanted to disappear, to wake from the dream on my bed in Achmetha. "You're shaking," Mandy whispered. "Amy, this isn't like you."

Was I being ridiculous? All girls married. *But not all girls take care of their father and sister for nine years.* I was six when Mother died, and Father wanted to join her. He laid in his bed for weeks while I took care of Mandy. Only when Grandfather threatened to remove us from Father's household did he finally return to life in our world. It was then that I begged him to begin my sword training—so I could be near him—to make sure the Medes' mightiest warrior regained his strength. The councilmen's wives cared for Mandy, taught her to spin, weave, and sew—and made her everything a wife should be. I was made a warrior.

Pressing the heels of my hands against both eyes, I refused to shed a tear. I scooted away from my sister, sniffing back snarled emotions and rising on my knees to see the city of which legends were born. Nearly every nation and tribe included Babylon as its place of origin, paying homage to a god-of-gods from whom all gods emerged. The ancients called him Enki. Phoenicians called him Bel. Babylonians worshipped his son, Marduk, and created a legend about a tall tower whose foundations reached into the earth's foundations. Marduk slayed the dread-god Tiamat, and humanity was born. The tower was the single line at the center of the world where heaven met earth.

A Jerusalem king of old—said to be wiser than any other—spun a similar tale about Babylon's ancient tower. Different, however, because it was humanity's quest to build the tower, to connect earth to only one god in heaven. In order to stymy the tower's completion, the nameless god confused their language, and in that moment nations came into being. Languages were created. And peoples spread over the earth. The tower endured through kings and kingdoms, from days of Chaldeans through Babylon's new day under King Nabopolassar's rule. He'd begun rebuilding the tower called Etemenanki, and I caught my first glimpse of it as our caravan left behind the dusty desert and descended onto a lush green plain.

"A...Am...y." My sister cried weakly behind me, stealing my attention. I turned and saw her collapse onto the pillows, her face blood-red but lips as white as milk.

"Father!" I screamed and then reached for our camel's reins and the riding crop. "I'll only swat you if your refuse to run," I promised the beast. Pulling her out of line, I gave a single, "Hyah!" and a gentle shake of the reins. Our camel commenced a long-legged mad dash that covered twice the distance of a galloping horse. I held tight to Mandy and the sedan sides.

Father's expression changed from anger to concern as we neared the front of the processional where he and Grandfather rode with their royal guards. Grandfather's face retained his perpetual scowl.

"It's Mandy," I said as the camel matched the pace of the co-rulers' stallions. "I think she's fainted from the heat, and I'm out of water." Without hesitation or questions, Father tossed me his waterskin.

I dampened the cloth I'd been using and laid it on her forehead while pouring a slight trickle from the skin directly into her mouth. "Come on, Mandy," I whispered. "Swallow."

"Get back in line before they see you." Grandfather's low growl lifted my eyes, and I saw Babylonian soldiers approaching —less than ten camel-lengths away. I started counting them. Ten. Twenty. Twenty-five.

"It's too late," Father whispered. "Let them see you caring for your sister, but Amy..." He fell silent until I met his gaze. "Do not speak. Hear me, girl, and obey."

I nodded, too terrified by the approaching Babylonians to

trust my voice. The entire contingent rode white stallions, five men in each row, two men leading. All wore full armor and weapons: leather breastplates and helmets, swords, spears, and bows. When they halted mere cubits from us, the lead rider on the left appeared of an age between my father and grandfather. Black-and-gray hair fell to his shoulders from beneath a helmet decorated with gold leaves and jewels. When my appraisal shifted to the horseman on his right, a young man only a few years older than I stared at me as if I were a rodent in his grain.

"Welcome to my kingdom, mighty kings of the Medes." King Nabopolassar wore a smirk and nodded in my direction. "Should I assume one of the young women on the camel is my son's intended bride?"

Mandy chose that moment to revive, gasping when she opened her eyes to the sight of a Babylonian army so near. "Oohh!" And with that single exclamation, her eyes rolled back, and she once again fainted into my arms.

"Mandy," I whispered, wiping her forehead with the cloth.

"Hmm," the younger man said. "I see little hope for a marriage if the fragile bride can't even withstand Babylon's heat in a covered sedan. Empty the waterskin over hear head," he commanded me. "She'll come around."

"I'll have you know—"

"My younger daughter, Mandane," Father said, cowing my angry retort, "has always been more delicate than Princess Amyitis—the daughter betrothed to Prince Nebuchadnezzar." He motioned toward me, and heat warmer than Babylon's summer rose in my cheeks.

"I am Nebuchadnezzar," he said, focused on me. "Perhaps Princess Amyitis would like to reconsider the betrothal." I held his gaze, matching his defiance.

"She does not reconsider." Father's tone brooked no argument.

Still I glared at the arrogant prince, my humiliation

demanding a reply. "Since I am only a woman and don't wish to further detract from this auspicious joining of the Babylonian and Median royalty, I'll send a messenger after we've been settled into our lodgings with my terms by which Prince Nebuchadnezzar may withdraw the betrothal if he so wishes."

Without waiting for his reply, I emptied Father's waterskin on Mandy's head. She bolted upright, gasping for air, and I turned her around so neither of Media's princesses need face the disdain of Babylon's prince.

The impromptu bath kept Mandy lucid until we arrived at the palace, where we were assigned separate chambers. Servants immediately placed my woozy sister in a cool bath, and I left her in capable hands to send the most important message of my life. Father burst into my chamber after he and Grandfather coordinated a plan for tonight's banquet—no doubt, hoping to intercept my message to the prince.

He was too late.

"If I'm old enough to marry, I can certainly send a private message to my betrothed."

"Your willful disobedience could endanger our whole nation, Amyitis. This is not a game!"

"No, it's my life!"

He grabbed my head, so angry I thought he might crush my skull. Instead, he stepped close and whispered with frightening calm. "I love you more than my own life, Amy, but I am first of all king and *secondly* your father. If you ruin this alliance with Babylon, I won't let Cyaxares punish you. I'll kill you myself." He kissed my forehead and hurried out the door. I didn't try to stop him.

Too anxious to rest, I surveyed the chamber furnishings and opened the heavy curtains drawn across my balcony. The city itself was stunning. A network of canals ran alongside mud-bricked streets, connecting every citizen to the great Euphrates that intersected the city beside the sacred tower we'd come to celebrate. The Etemananki was beyond spectacular, higher than any building I'd ever seen and more glorious than other temples. As I watched Babylon from my balcony, pulsing with life, commerce, and growth, I could almost believe it was the center of the world.

"Mistress?" Startled, I instinctively drew my dagger on a serving maid no older than Mandy. She clutched a purple gown to her chest and said, "I can leave if you wish."

"I brought my own clothes." She gulped, and I sheathed my dagger, feeling guilty for my ungratefulness. "Thank you for bringing the gown, but I don't have a maid at home, and I'm perfectly capable of dressing myself."

She bowed, remaining rooted to the floor. "The gown has the coveted color wrought only from the mullex shells of Tyre. It's a gift from the crown prince, and he would be most displeased if you refuse it." She held out a small scroll. "He sent you this message and made me promise that no one but you would see it."

I snatched it from her hand, broke the seal, and read:

Father said I must apologize for my rude greeting, so I hope you like the gown. I've never been challenged to match swords with a girl, but it will provide jovial dinner entertainment for tonight's banquet. I accept your proposal. The winner determines the fate of our betrothal without affecting the outcome of our nations' alliance. You are a strange girl.

I crumbled up the parchment. Strange girl. He was the most arrogant man on earth. I smiled sweetly at the maid. "You may stay and help me prepare for the banquet." I walked over to my basket of personal belongings, and lifted out my sword. "I'll be wearing this as an ornament on my belt. Do sapphires or pearls look best with Hittite iron and Tyrian purple?"

THREE

"The proud and arrogant person—'Mocker' is his name—
behaves with insolent fury."
Proverbs 21:24

Same Evening

I'd been sitting on the same stool since just after midday, and now the stars twinkled brightly overhead. "How can there be room for any more paint on my face?" I couldn't see the stars, of course, since my eyes were closed to receive green malachite powder on my lids.

"There," she said, sounding pleased. "Finished."

My hands balled into fists in my lap. "I can't believe I forgot my hand mirror." I was equally annoyed that the Babylonians would place a princess in a chamber without a full-length mirror—without *any* mirror! I bolted off my stool and stood over the maid. "How do I know if my appearance is adequate for the banquet?"

Her forehead wrinkled as if I'd asked why the sky was blue. "You'll be the most beautiful woman in the room, Mistress."

Her round eyes blinked with a coyness that unnerved me. I lifted my hand to the precious stones woven into my hair and piled atop my head. I looked down at the deep purple linen that draped my curves and felt Mother's sapphire necklace around my neck. The girl had even polished the hilt of my sword and oiled its leather belt. She'd lined my eyes with kohl, applied red ochre to my lips and cheeks. She stared at me now with a quizzical tilt of her head, and suddenly I knew—she'd been sent to ruin me. I'd been given no mirror so I couldn't see the mockery she'd made of me.

"Leave." Her features clouded, but she bowed and retreated without a word. I gripped the balcony railing, refusing to let my tears overflow. I'd never been the most beautiful girl in any room. Babylon's crown prince had probably sent her as an agent of humiliation to make a fool of me.

My chamber door slammed shut, and I was glad she was gone. I even considered running inside to lock it, washing my face, and changing into my sparring robe. But Grandfather would kill me. Worse, Father would be shamed. Nebuchadnezzar had won. Before I even drew my sword, he'd bested me.

"Amy?" I turned to the sound of Father's voice, and his expression confirmed my fears. His mouth opened. Closed. Opened. "You look…"

"Ridiculous." I tried to storm past him, but he caught my arm, still staring. "Amyitis, you're stunning." I tried to cover my face but he pulled my hands away—and kissed them before twining my arm with his and leading me to the door. "I checked on Mandy," he said, "but she's still too weakened by the travel and heat to attend the banquet. She'll be sad she missed seeing you like this."

Father's royal guard waited in the hall to escort us, and all ten men gawked like I wore no gown at all. Did I really look so different?

"Perhaps I'll stop and see Mandy after the banquet." I

doubted I'd be allowed to remain after I sparred with Babylon's crown prince. Both my Elamite and Persian suitors dismissed me immediately after my sword sent them to their knees. The thought of doing so to Nebuchadnezzar restored a little bounce to my step.

"Oh no!" I stopped mid-stride and pulled Father aside. Our guards formed a human shield while I lifted my gown to show him my bare feet. His resonant laughter drew the attention of guests entering the banquet hall, no more than a stone's throw away, and I swatted his arm. "Don't laugh! I have to go back for my sandals."

"No, little warrior." He positioned my sword on my left hip and smiled down with sparkling eyes. "Your husband will meet you just as you are."

My throat tightened, regretting the secret I'd kept from him. Would he be terribly angry about the sparring match? Before I could confess, we were on our way again, and too soon I was walking down the center aisle of Babylon's throne hall. The banquet noise wound down the way a child's top slowly ceases spinning. Grandfather sat beside King Nabopolassar at a table on the elevated dais and looked up when the crowd began to quiet. Still scowling, he watched our approach with a level of interest I'd seldom garnered.

The crown prince sat on the other side of his father, and two younger men—certainly his brothers because of the resemblance—sat at Nebuchadnezzar's left. He glanced our way at first, then started to return to his conversation with his brothers, but looked back at me with eyes as large as my faithful camel's. He stood slowly, frozen, with an expression hard to decipher. One of his brothers nudged him, and the crown prince descended the steps to await our arrival in a cleared space in front of the dais. The room was completely still.

Father halted an arm's length from him. "I present your bride, Crown Prince Nebuchadnezzar. She is the Medes' most beautiful woman, my daughter, Amyitis." Father lifted my hand from his arm, kissed it, and offered it to the prince. "You may call her Amy."

"You may call me Amyitis." Fire rushed into my cheeks when Nebuchadnezzar grasped my hand, his eyes boring into mine like they would steal my soul.

"She's beautiful indeed, King Astyages, and a mystery."

Father ascended the steps, and I wanted to rush after him. Instead I turned from the intensity of the prince's gaze to face an audience of a thousand Babylonians. I felt safer.

Nebuchadnezzar released my hand. "Princess Amyitis and I have arranged a special event for your entertainment." His voice was so deep it rattled my chest, and when he drew his sword, a curious buzz stirred among the guests. "Who in this room would be foolish enough to resist a betrothal with a princess as beautiful as Amyitis?"

Laughter replaced the silence, and battle lust replaced my angst. "And what princess could refuse such a virile prince?" Like lightning, I drew my sword and nicked his right cheek, shocking the guests and infuriating the royals behind us.

Nebuchadnezzar calmed his father, chuckling while he dabbed blood from his cheek. "Amy and I are the future of our nations. We are agreed that an alliance between the Medes and Babylonians is a positive step for both kingdoms, but it is the winner of our sparring match who will decide if our betrothal joins our households." He raised his voice for the whole crowd to hear. "Let our sparring demonstrate that a Babylonian and Mede can fight *together* and maintain independence." He returned his attention to me and winked.

His condescension heightened my fury, and when Nabopolassar said, "Don't hurt her, Neb," I briskly nicked the prince's left cheek. The second cut doused his good humor, and he charged at me like every other muscle-bound, over-confident warrior. My last-minute slide to the right left him lunging at air.

I twirled, drew my dagger, and sliced his sword belt before he realized it was falling to the floor.

He peered down at the leather strip gathered around his ankles and then up at me. I waited for the fury that pushed my other suitors to their final foolish mistakes, but Nebuchadnezzar did something far more unsettling.

"It would seem I've underestimated my opponent," he announced to the crowd. "To win Amy's heart, I'll have to do more than cross swords."

To win my heart?

My momentary distraction let him tip my sword and send it clattering to the floor. I lunged with my dagger, but he grabbed my wrist, whirled me around, and trapped me against his chest. He bent over my shoulder and whispered, "You are magnificent." Then, pressing gently against the small bones of my wrist, he shook my hand to dislodge the dagger—sealing my defeat in less than three heartbeats. The banquet hall erupted in whistles and cheers. Cymbals and drums led the musicians in festive tunes since the early entertainment had finished so quickly. And my captor lingered in the victor's pose.

I grew suddenly aware of his nearness, never having been so close to a man. Utterly still in his arms, I felt the tingle of his left arm around my stomach, pulling me against him. His right hand still held my wrist against my shoulder while his muscular arm wrapped high across my chest. Like a baby bird, wrapped in its mother's wings, I was engulfed by the enormity of his presence. He could have harmed me but hadn't. He could have humiliated me but he refrained. Could he truly think me worthy of betrothal?

As if sensing my unease, he slowly released his grasp but cradled my hand as he turned us to face our fathers. "King Astyages, as the victor of tonight's sparring, I have one request before making the decision about our betrothal." I held my breath and realized too late I was squeezing his hand. He smiled and held me with his eyes while asking my father, "May I invite Princess Amyitis to my chamber in the morning to break our fast together—privately—before making my decision."

I didn't hear Father's answer. I only know Nebuchadnezzar's eyes never left mine until he leaned over, brushing his lips against my ear. "I'll send a guard to escort you to my chamber in the morning."

I nodded, unable to speak, and turned to walk up the aisle toward the rear doors. I needed to see Mandy. To tell her I didn't frighten away my suitor. To tell her he thought me magnificent. To tell her—perhaps I could marry after all.

FOUR

"He who finds a wife finds what is good
and receives favor from the Lord."
Proverbs 18:22

Next Morning

I f I married Nebuchadnezzar, would Mandy see the same sun rising in Achmetha that I watched from Babylon? This morning, I watched the eastern horizon slowly change from deep purple, to amethyst, to lavender, while contemplating the thousand other questions she'd asked me last night—for which I had no answers. The Medes didn't educate women. I knew how to read and write but only because I'd asked Father to teach me. I knew nothing compared to Babylonian women who were educated alongside their brothers. They learned literature, geography, mathematics, and even the art and science of the stars.

He'll think me an ignorant Mede. I'd known about the Etemenanki—the tower between heaven and earth—because Father knew King Nabopolassar planned to begin its restoration while we were in Babylon and thought I should be conversant in its details. Mandy suggested I speak with Nebuchadnezzar about it this morning, but what should I say? I knew only how to swing a sword. I hated to spin and weave and sew. I couldn't sing or play a musical instrument. *What if I'm barren?* These thoughts and more had robbed my sleep and convinced me I should save Babylon's crown prince from making the most dire mistake of his life.

I couldn't marry him. If he pressed the betrothal, I would refuse. It was the kindest thing I could do for the man who had been most kind to me. It was kindness I saw in his eyes last night. Only kindness. Wasn't it?

A knock on my door made me jump like a desert hare. I shot off my couch, wrapped in a thin blanket, hair and face blissfully free of last night's attempted beauty. Though Mandy had been complimentary of the maid's efforts, I felt almost deceptive under the mask of finery. Another knock, this one louder and longer, hurried my pace.

"I'm coming!" I opened the door and found two guards and the wide-eyed maid I'd treated so rudely last night. I reached for her hand, drawing her into the chamber. "I'm so glad you came back. I wanted to apologize for the way I—"

"Good morning, Princess Amyitis." The guards bowed in unison. "Prince Nebuchadnezzar requests the honor of your presence to break your fast together."

I wasn't sure which one spoke but was certain I'd misunderstood. "You mean he'd like me to *prepare* to meet him?" Perhaps he really had sent the maid this time.

Both guards rose, and one met my gaze. "No, my lady. He requests we escort you to his chamber immediately."

"It's barely past dawn."

"Indeed," the other guard said. "And he commanded us to emphasize that he displayed remarkable restraint in waiting so long."

I covered an unsanctioned giggle and found the maid grinning too. "I was assigned to your chamber again this morning, Mistress, and found the guards already at your door when I arrived."

He didn't send her this time either. I appraised my appearance but, in the absence of a mirror, I needed some help. Stepping back, I dropped the blanket to the floor, turned in a full circle, and shrugged. "It's better he realize I'm not much of a prize after all." Both guards shifted uncomfortably, and one even started to respond. I saved him the forced compliment. "Let me at least comb my hair. I'll be right out."

The maid followed me inside and shut the door behind us. Combing my hair was just an excuse to strap my dagger to my left thigh—just in case. I started toward the door, but the maid blocked my path. "You aren't really going like that, are you?"

Still wearing my purple gown, I was at least clothed in respectable attire. "Why wouldn't I? Perhaps this will convince Babylon's future king that he needs a better wife than me." She looked so sad I hugged her and whispered, "Thank you for making me feel beautiful for one night."

I hurried out the door and followed the guards through a labyrinth of back staircases and winding halls. Feeling more uneasy about being a foreign princess escorted by guards I didn't know, I was suddenly happy I'd brought my dagger. We emerged through a doorway into an ornately decorated hall where six royal guards stood at attention by two chambers. As we approached, one guard pounded the head of his spear against the door on his left and then opened it without invitation.

I stopped, a quiet gasp escaping at the sight of Nebuchadnezzar in a loose-fitting linen robe, hands clasped behind his back. In that moment, I was ruined. My heart was bound to him as we appraised each other. I wanted nothing more than to feel his arms around me as they'd been last night. To feel his breath on my cheek. The exquisite agony when he released me but still held my hand.

I looked down, glimpsing my bare feet, and the reality of my inadequacy loosened my tongue. "I'm honored that you would keep your promise though I wish to release you from the obligation. We need not break our fast together—"

"I thought we'd be more comfortable in the temple courtyard." In three strides he was at my side, arm circling my waist, and fairly carrying me while I tried to keep up. He focused straight ahead as he spoke, his words tumbling out at the same pace with which we sped through the palace. "I've thought of nothing but the betrothal all night, Amy. We'll tell our fathers that we won't wait a full year. Why wait when I leave for the Nineveh campaign next month. We'll pay whatever bride price your father names and have your wedding garments fitted by the new moon festival next week."

"Wait!" I said as we emerged from the palace into the morning air.

He looked as startled as I felt and cupped my face in his large hands. "By the gods, Amyitis, Princess of the Medes, I cannot *wait*. When I see what I want, I must have it." He brushed a kiss across my lips. "You are what I want."

Eyes closed, I felt as if the ground beneath me shifted, and my chest ached with a strange new feeling. I opened my eyes and saw the longing returned. Could it even be love?

Stark terror shot through me like lightning. Shoving him away, I turned and fled down the palace steps, running aimlessly. Blinding tears stole my dignity, erupting in irrepressible sobs. Giant arms captured me from behind, and though I fought them at first, I finally surrendered to the compassion they offered.

"You'll leave me." I buried my face against his shoulder. "I'm not a woman you can love, and you won't look at me the same way when you know me."

He didn't answer, and I was almost relieved that he'd offered no resistance. Almost. It might have been nice if he'd argued a little. Keeping my eyes closed and my face hidden in his collar, I drank in the scent of him. Frankincense and the musky hint of juniper. I'd never forget the feel of being carried like a leaf carried on the wind.

When he stopped, he set me on my feet and tugged my hand gently to sit on the lush green grass beside him. Again, his stare was so intense, I had to look away. "I will not beg you to marry me," he said, "but neither will I be told who I will love."

My tears betrayed me again, and I couldn't speak.

"Look at me, Amyitis."

I owed him that much. Our eyes met, but I felt as if his eyes might mine the deepest secrets of my soul. Beyond unnerving, it was rude. "Why can't you simply believe me? You would grow tired of a woman like me."

"There are no other women like you!" He shouted, gaining the attention of two bald priests.

I looked around, suddenly realizing we sat in the grassy courtyard of the Etemenanki. Tipping my head back, I shaded my eyes from the morning sun to inspect the highest ziggurat I'd ever seen. If this was the place where heaven met earth, surely the gods could help this stubborn prince grasp why we should never marry.

When I returned my attention to him, he was smiling. "You see? Any other woman would have dissolved into tears when I shouted at her—or perhaps gotten angry."

"If you shout about something I don't like, I'll get angry." Perhaps I needed to clarify. "When you said there were no other women like me, were you attempting to compliment me?"

He laughed and threw himself back on the grass. "Amy, you must marry me!"

"Shh!" I pressed my hand over his mouth, noticing sidelong glances from a growing number of priests.

He leaned on one elbow and captured my hand, kissing my palm. Fire raced up my arm as his gaze softened. "I will love you my whole life, Amyitis. Nothing you say can change that."

"I don't know how to spin or weave or sew." It sounded silly when I said it aloud. "And I don't know how to play a musical instrument. I'd make a terrible queen."

"You most certainly make a terrible liar." He sat up and rested his forearms on his knees. "Tell me the real reason you're afraid to marry me."

"Afraid?" How dare he. "I'm not afra—" I was afraid. I hated cowards, and I hated *being* afraid even more.

He brushed my cheek with the back of his knuckles—the same way Father showed me he cared. "Tell me what frightens you, Amy. I'll fight for you."

I'll fight for you. How could he fight my own insecurities? "I'm not smart, Nebuchadnezzar. I can read and write, but I'm not educated like the beautiful women that surround you." I pulled at the grass, refusing to see pity in his eyes. "And I'm not strong enough to endure your rejection."

He sat in silence for the span of several heartbeats which was far worse than his shouting. Finally, he stood, and I was certain he'd leave me to find my own way back to the palace.

His hand brushed my cheek again and lingered in invitation. "Come with me, Amy. I want to show you something." I took his hand, and he led me into the Etemenanki. Brick layers and engravers worked feverishly all around us. I felt like a naughty child—like when Mandy and I snuck into the stables to pet Father's prized stallion—but Nebuchadnezzar held his head high, and the priests bowed to him as we passed.

He paused at the entrance to a winding staircase. "Medes are known for tenacity. Are you a true Mede, Amyitis?"

I lowered my head, letting him think I was considering the question—and then raced past him up the steps. He roared behind me as we climbed the stairway to heaven, leaving the cares of earth behind. Legs aching, lungs burning, I could barely lift my feet to summit the final steps. Even Babylon's prince pressed both hands on the stair-well walls as he pushed himself up the last step to join me on the small platform on top of the world.

I clung to him, terrified to look over the edge. He held me close and pressed a kiss atop my head. "Some of the best soldiers in my royal guard can't make that climb, Amy. I sent for you this morning at dawn to see if you would come as you were—without the feminine trappings of jewels and paints. You came. Barefooted even."

"I hate sandals," I said. "I was barefooted last night too. You just didn't notice." His laughter rumbled against my cheek, and I snuggled into him. "I'm also wearing a dagger on my left thigh under this lovely purple dress. But the things you find intriguing now, Nebuchadnezzar, will become an annoyance."

"I'm sure they will," he said, nudging me away to look me in the eyes again. "But I won't allow you to be defeated by your own limitations. You will learn to spin, weave, sew, and play a musical instrument. And I will make sure you're educated by the finest teachers in Babylon. You'll learn everything you wish to know, Amy. Do you hear me?"

I wasn't sure if I should be offended at his presumption or overwhelmed by his generosity. Before I could respond, a shadow darkened his features. "But you must understand the challenges of marrying the future king of Babylon."

I almost listed the *challenges* I'd learned since meeting him yesterday. Arrogant. Bossy. Impatient. But he was too serious for any jesting.

"I'm a warrior who will lead my army to faraway battles for long stretches of time. I'm arrogant. I'm stubborn. And I don't share my treasure. You will be mine, Amyitis. If another man looks at you with longing, I'll take his eyes. If he speaks flirtations, I'll take out his tongue. If another man shows you affection, I'll dig out his heart with a trowel."

"I hope we have only daughters," I said, "for a loving son would wander this earth blind, mute, and heartless."

He grinned and straightened to full height, pointing to a small tent near the northern edge of the platform. "When I am king," he said soberly, "I will spend one night each year in that tent with a priestess." He searched my expression. "It is my duty as king to share my seed and ensure a plentiful harvest."

I knew what the gods demanded of kings. Grandfather did it. Father too. I hated the thought of my husband in that tent with a priestess, but my life was lived with kings. His duty to the nation would always come first.

"I...I..." I had no more excuses. The realization settled into my spirit—I would soon be his wife.

Cradling my head, he slid his fingers into the back of my hair and drew so close that our noses nearly touched. "Tell me, Amy. What else should I know of you before you become my wife?"

His wife. The joy of it began to grow and the reality that he truly could love me—me—settled into my soul. What kind of wife would I be? Looking into his eyes, this time I matched his intensity without apology or trepidation. "I will not be tamed, but I will obey. I will not be humiliated, but I choose to serve you. I will not be ignored, but I'll make you ache to be in my presence." I cradled his head the same way he held mind and pulled him into a timid kiss—and then smiled sheepishly. "Only one thing I request, and I will not be denied."

He licked his lips like a hungry jackal. "Name it."

"I must return to my precious Zagros Mountains for the summer months. Babylon is a smelting oven, and I need to spend time with my sister."

Like dousing a fire with a pail of water, his smile disappeared. Would he refuse me? Why should he care that I returned to Achmetha if he was off fighting a war in Nineveh or Phoenicia or Canaan or Egypt? His fingers tightened in my hair, and he drew my head back slightly to expose my neck. Then he placed a trail of kisses from my ear to my shoulder. "You may spend your summers in Achmetha only if I'm welcome to visit any time I please."

Our negotiations were over, and I was the victor. "I am yours, Crown Prince Nebuchadnezzar. We have sealed the alliance of our nations."

PART II

DANIEL –
MY ABBA, MY HERO

FIVE

"The sons of Josiah: Johanan the firstborn, [Eliakim] the second son,
[Mattaniah] the third, Shallum the fourth."
1 Chronicles 3:13

31st year of Josiah's reign - Ab (July) — Jerusalem — Atarah

I rose on tip-toes, sliding my fingers into the silky curls at the back of Johanan's head, and held on tight. "You will defeat Pharaoh Neco's troops and come back to me."

His lazy grin still made my heart flutter. "Yes, Commander Atarah." He wrapped one arm around my waist and pulled me into him, kissing me with a longing that terrified me.

I pushed him away. "That wasn't an I'll-come-back kiss." Swiping at stubborn tears, I lodged my fists on both hips. "That was an I'm-not-sure-Abba-Josiah's-decision-is-a-good-one kiss."

"Atarah." He walked toward the balcony with a sigh, massaging the back of his neck. "Abba believes if Judah can stop

Egypt's troops from joining Assyria, Babylon might overthrow Assyria—and bring the empire to its knees."

"Would a new Babylonian Empire be any better?" I'd heard awful things about Babylon's young general, Prince Nebuchadnezzar. "And if Judah's army is decimated while trying to delay Egypt's troops, wouldn't it mean the crumbling of all your abba Josiah has rebuilt?" My voice broke, but I fought to regain control. Johanan was a soldier and responded to reason, not a wife's emotional pleas. "Why won't your abba let you—his crown prince—remain here, instead of placing your youngest brother on the throne? He isn't even married. He still summons Hamutal to his chamber when he's ill. She spoons broth into his mouth like he's a child."

"My ima would still feed *me* broth if I'd let her." Johanan chuckled, and I couldn't deny the truth. Hamutal doted on all three of her sons—though my husband was the only honorable man among them.

He pulled me close again, staring too long before he spoke. "If something happens to both Abba and me, Atarah—"

"No!"

I tried to pull away, but his grip on me tightened. "Listen, Wife—for Daniel's sake."

Our son's name ceased my struggle and forced a prayer. *Yahweh, please. I can't lose this man. He's my breath, my life.* I nestled against his chest, taking shelter in the strong frame that had been my protection since I was fourteen.

"I suspect Mattaniah and Shallum secretly worship pagan gods." He paused, waiting for me to react, but I said nothing. I suspected Hamutal herself had led her younger sons into idolatry. Johanan's half-brother as well. "Though Judah would change under their rule, their respect for our ima would keep you and Daniel alive."

"Alive?" I looked up, startled at the thought of danger to our son. "Of course we'd be safe if one of your brothers—"

"You won't be safe if Eliakim sits on Abba's throne, my love. You know how his ima and mine have competed since he was born only a few months after me. If Eliakim sits on Judah's throne, you and Daniel must leave Jerusalem quickly and go to Ima Hamutal's relatives in Libnah."

"But our son should sit on Judah's thro—"

"That's why he's not safe, Atarah." Eyes flashing, voice sharp, it was then I realized the depth of my husband's fear. A knock on our chamber doused his angst. "I asked his maid to bring him. Come!" he shouted, moving toward the door.

"Abba!" Our four-year-old ran into Johanan's arms, wooden sword in hand. "I want to fight Egyptians. Can I go? Pleeeease!"

"Absolutely not!" I said, glaring at my husband. "Where did he even hear about—"

To my horror, Johanan drew his dagger and began sparring with our son. "You can't come on this campaign, but continue sword drills with your cousins and friends and you'll become a warrior king like Saba Josiah." With a false left jab at Daniel's ribs, he somehow tipped the wooden sword into the air and sheathed his blade in a single fluid motion.

Our wide-eyed son watched his sword fall to the floor, while Johanan swooped him up into his arms. A tickling frenzy ensued, and Johanan fell onto our bed with our sandy-haired boy. How could a man the size of a bear be as gentle as a lamb? Yet it was one of the things I loved most about my husband.

"All right," I said, playing the family villain. "We must finish filling Abba's shoulder bag before his regiment comes to collect their general."

Johanan tossed Daniel over his shoulder like a sack of grain and stood, mischief lighting his dark-brown eyes. "Did I hear your ima say *she* wanted to be tickled, Daniel? Is that what she said?"

"Yes, Abba!" He cackled. "That's what she said!"

"No!" I scampered around the bed. "Johanan ben Josiah, don't you dare."

He set Daniel's feet on the tiled floor, and they converged like jackals on prey, tickling me mercilessly until we all three crumpled to the floor in a heap of love and laughter. When the nearness had sufficiently soothed our hearts, we lay spent, I in the bend of Johanan's arm and Daniel pillowed on his opposite shoulder.

"While I'm gone, Daniel," Johanan said, "I'm entrusting Ima to your care."

Our darling boy sat up, straight as a measuring rod. "I will, Abba." He jumped to his feet and ran for his sword, returning to hold it high. "I'll even fight off Philistines if they come."

I covered a grin, but Johanan sat up, his expression all too serious. He pressed our son's sword to his side and thumped his forehead. "Use your mind, Daniel. A wise man can defeat his enemy far more often than a man skilled with a sword. When danger comes, Yahweh will show you what to do."

Eyes rounded, Daniel nodded. "Hananiah's abba is teaching me lots of things, Abba. I'm a good student."

Johanan pulled him into a fierce hug, blinking away tears. "Hananiah and his abba are good people, good friends. Learn well, my son. Yahweh will care for you when I'm gone."

When I'm gone? I stumbled back when Johanan rose to embrace me. "You're coming back," I whispered.

He nodded and I wrapped my arms around his waist, memorizing everything. His smell, his strong arms, the sound of his heartbeat, the length of his breaths.

"I must go, Atarah."

Reluctantly, I loosened my grip and picked up my son, laying my head against his chest.

"When will abba come back?" he asked as we watched our lives walk away.

"I don't know, love, but we'll see him again someday."

Please, Yahweh, don't make me wait until Paradise.

SIX

"While Josiah was king, Pharaoh Necho king of Egypt went up to
the Euphrates River to help the king of Assyria.
King Josiah marched out to meet him in battle,
but Necho faced him and killed him at Megiddo."
2 Kings 23:29

Tishri (October) — Jerusalem

Hamutal's mourning wail split the peaceful dawn like a spear through my heart. Running from my chamber, the chamber guards two doors from mine stood at the threshold, gawking inside. When I rounded the corner, a messenger knelt beside Hamutal, King Josiah's first wife and Johanan's ima. She was prostrate on the floor with a crumpled parchment beside her. The messenger looked at me, his expression a mixture of grief and pity.

When the man looked at a second sealed parchment and started toward me, I knew my world was forever changed. With the timidity of a frightened beast, he approached and offered the small scroll from a trembling hand. "May Yahweh help us all, Mistress Atarah." He bowed and left me with a message I didn't want and a queen I couldn't console.

Hamutal's wailing moved to the edges of my consciousness as the scroll in my hand pulled me to my knees. Shaking violently, I noted the wax seal of Johanan's half-brother, Eliakim. Son of Josiah's second wife, Zebidah. I broke the seal and unfurled the small parchment.

Johanan dead. Abba mortally wounded. Many will die if Shallum takes my throne.

My gut roiled and I crumbled the message, too panicked to wail. Somehow, Johanan knew Eliakim would challenge Shallum for the throne. He'd tried to prepare me. I found my voice and fumbled to my feet. "Hamutal, we must get Daniel and go to your relatives in Libnah." She was oblivious to me. "Hamutal!" I tried again, shaking her shoulder.

This time she paused, her eyes focusing. "Josiah. Johanan. Gone."

Face twisting into the horror of loss, she tried to bury her cries in her folded arms, but I lifted her shoulders, helping her to stand. "Ima Hamutal, please. Johanan told me before he left to keep Daniel safe. If Eliakim returns to take the throne—"

"He will not take the throne!" Suddenly alert, she bolted to her feet. "Josiah left my Shallum on the throne, and on the throne he'll stay." Like a slap to her face, years of harem battles staunched her tears. "I should speak with the royal council before Zebidah hears the news. Josiah chose Shallum to sit on Judah's throne, not her son."

"Yes, but we must—"

She was out the door before I could beg her to consider Daniel's safety first. How could we flee to Libnah if Hamutal was determined to guard Shallum's right to the throne in Jerusalem? I'd only met her Libnah relatives at our wedding ten years ago. How could I travel over the mountains with a four-year-old—so close to Philistine territory?

"Ima?" My son and his maid stood at the open doorway. "Why is everyone crying?"

The maid's face was the color of goat's milk. "I took him to your chamber when we heard the mourners' wailing spread, Mistress." She looked at the crumpled parchment still in my hand. "Is it...is it bad?"

Fighting hysteria, I pressed my lips together and looked to the ceiling in hopes of gaining enough control to tell my son his world was shattered. A little hand slipped around mine, dismantling any hope of restrained emotion. I covered a sob and knelt to face my little man.

"Your saba Josiah and abba were brave warriors and fought the Egyptians to protect us, but they were both killed during the battle, Daniel."

Dark eyebrows pulled together, creating two deep creases above his button nose. "Who will lead our soldiers if both Saba and Abba are dead?"

Leave it to the son of the crown prince to think of Judah first. "Each regiment has a captain to lead them, and Dohd Eliakim will lead the royal guard."

His eyes began to fill. "If they're dead, I won't get to see them anymore. Right?"

"Not while we live here. But we'll see them again in Paradise."

"But that's a long time," he said, hugging my neck, letting his tears turn to sobs. "I want to see them now." More wailing erupted down the hall, and Daniel squeezed me tighter. "I hate the screaming, Ima. Take me away from the screaming."

He was shaking now, growing hysterical. "Shh, love. It's mourners. They're grieving the loss of those who were killed in battle." More wailing began—this time the high-pitched shrieks of professional mourners.

Daniel covered his ears. "Nooo! Make them stop!" Stomping and screaming, he grew inconsolable.

Scooping him into my arms, I ran down the harem stairway and through the main hallway, toward the palace classroom where Daniel met daily with other royal and noblemen's sons. Though it was too early for Master Enoch and the other boys to be there, perhaps the sound of mourners would be muffled by the distance from the harem.

When we crossed the threshold, Daniel's crying lessened. He still held me tightly but sobbed quietly against my shoulder. "Shh, we must grieve Saba Josiah and Abba for thirty days, love. The mourners are paid to wail."

"I will grieve longer than that," he said, sniffing. "And I'll do it quieter without pay."

I chuckled, squeezing him closer. "Yes, I know you will."

"We must leave the palace, Ima."

His declaration startled me. Had he heard of Eliakim's threat? He hadn't been in the room when Johanan had warned me to take him to Libnah if Eliakim ruled. "Why must we leave the palace, Daniel?"

"I can't listen to the mourners for thirty days."

My eyes slid shut. Perhaps the mourners were Yahweh's gift so my son would at least be willing to leave his friends and family behind. "I'm trying to find a way to Libnah—"

He squirmed out of my arms and looked up at me. "We can't leave Jerusalem, Ima."

His matter-of-fact declaration disarmed me. "It might not be safe for us to stay, Daniel. Abba would want me to keep you safe."

"Abba told me to keep *you* safe. Remember, Ima?"

"I remember, but—"

"We'll live with Master Enoch's family," he said as if I were a slow student. "You and Mistress Hobah are friends."

My immediate response was to dismiss the idea. My four-year-old simply wanted to live with his best friend, Hananiah. But in that infinitesimal moment before saying *no*, I considered the wisdom of his suggestion. The royal tutor's home was near the Corner Gate, far from the palace yet still in the Upper City. If Daniel and I remained in the palace while Shallum was on the throne, Eliakim would assume I'd ignored his message. If we lived with Enoch and Hobah, perhaps Eliakim would believe we moved *because* Shallum took the throne. We didn't need to speak the truth or a lie. Palace politics was all about what others *perceived*.

I knelt to meet my smart boy eye-to-eye. "You're doing a very good job of taking care of me. Now, let me give you all the grown-up facts so we can make this decision together." He nodded once and folded his arms across his chest, waiting for me to continue. "If your dohd Shallum rules Judah, we'll stay in Jerusalem. If the council chooses someone else, we'll take Savta Hamutal with us and go to Libnah."

"Savta Hamutal will make sure Dohd Shallum rules Judah."

I stood, offering my hand to him as I turned toward the door. "I'm afraid you're right, love. There aren't many men who refuse Queen Hamutal."

SEVEN

"Pharaoh Necho made Eliakim son of Josiah king in place of his father Josiah and changed Eliakim's name to Jehoiakim. But he took Jehoahaz and carried him off to Egypt, and there he died."
2 Kings 23:34

Tebeth (January)

Jerusalem had enjoyed relative peace since Mattaniah returned home with the hastily-wrapped bodies of Judah's king and crown prince three months ago. Bloodied and beaten troops, under the command of Josiah's third-born son, honored their fallen leaders and crept back to their homes, defeated and sullen. Mattaniah, relieved to let his younger brother rule, lived quietly in the palace with his wife and two sons.

Daniel and I settled into life with Enoch and Hobah's family, who treated us more like family than guests. Rather than being a nuisance, I became a much-needed extra pair of hands to tackle chores in a household that could only afford a single servant. A household with four active boys: two four-year-olds and twin two-year-olds. Daniel and Hananiah went to school six days a week with Enoch, leaving Hobah and me to wrestle the twins between daily chores.

The second day of every week we cleaned. Rugs. Bedding. Baskets. I was grateful for the distraction. Though not even busy hands could heal my broken heart. I ached for Johanan and still expected him to walk through a doorway a hundred times a day. The grief was infuriating. Taking another swing at the rug hanging on a hemp cord, I watched dust float on a morning breeze.

"Whose face are you imagining on that rug?" Hobah teased.

How could I explain that loss dismantles every emotion and rearranges it to look different than it's looked before? "I spoke with Hamutal yesterday. I think she finally believes me—that I moved out of the palace to protect Daniel, with no ill will toward Shallum—oops. I mean, King Jehoahaz." I stopped beating the rug and rolled my eyes at Hobah, still uncomfortable with the *throne name* given to Johanan's little brother.

She laughed, knowingly. I'd shared too many family stories for her to ever look at him with much respect. Our light-heartedness pricked my heart. I needed to tell her the real reason for my visit to the palace yesterday. Setting aside my stick, I reached for my friend's hand and drew her to a nearby bench to sit with me.

"You know how much I appreciate you and Enoch opening your home to Daniel and me."

Her face clouded. "You're not moving back to the palace."

"No, but I've asked Hamutal to write a recommendation for us to her relatives in Libnah." Hobah removed her hand from my grasp, but I snagged it back. "Listen to me! It's what Johanan wanted and the safest place for Daniel."

She turned away, but I could see by her profile she was

struggling not to cry. "We're your family now, Atarah. Why must you leave?"

Shofars sounded in the distance, pulling both of us to our feet. Hobah's frightened glance begged an explanation. "When I visited Hamutal," I said, "she'd heard reports that Eliakim's regiment would return soon. After the battle that killed Josiah and Johanan, Eliakim and his regiment pursued Pharaoh Necho's personal contingent north to seek revenge." Hobah's features twisted into disbelief. The report sounded as bogus today as when I heard it from Hamutal. Why would a prince of Judah lead his regiment into the jaws of a lion?

Shofars sounded a second time, and the rumble of the ground beneath us proved an army was approaching. "We should get to the palace to see what's happening." Hobah grabbed one of the twins, while I took the other and hurried out of their courtyard.

Shouldering through curious noblemen's families, we made our way to the palace and entered through the servants' quarters to avoid the crowd. Through a maze of hallways, we hurried down a side passage to our boys' classroom and found everyone peering out the wall of windows.

"I've never seen a pharaoh before," one boy said.

The boy beside him nudged him too hard. "That's not a pharaoh. Prince Eliakim would never lead a pharaoh into Jerusalem."

"Maybe Prince Eliakim likes Egyptians."

"That's treason." Eliakim's son balled his fist and hit the boy.

Enoch stepped between them and pulled them away from the windows. "We'll have no violence in my classroom. You will learn to defend yourselves with your minds, not with your fists."

Daniel and Hananiah saw us at the door, and both boys

shouted, "Ima!" running to wrap their arms around Hobah and me.

Enoch looked at me, concern creasing his brow. I crossed the room to look out the window—as quickly as possible with a two-year-old in my arms and my own four-year-old hugging my leg. Unfortunately, the boy was right. Prince Eliakim was indeed leading Pharaoh into Jerusalem. Both the prince and a man wearing a gleaming gold collar and Pschent—Egypt's double crown—approached the palace on matching white stallions.

How much should I disclose in a room full of princes' and noblemen's sons? I offered the only information of which I was certain. "Prince Eliakim and King Jehoahaz will sort this out. Until then, class is dismissed. Master Enoch and Mistress Hobah will escort you home." I lowered my voice for only Enoch to hear. "Take them out the servant's entrance. Avoid the main streets. I'm not sure what Eliakim has planned, but if he's brought Pharaoh Necho, I fear there may be a fight." I shifted his two-year-old son to his arms. "I'm going to the throne hall. Take Daniel home with you too."

"No, Ima." Daniel hugged my leg tighter, having overheard. "Abba said I'm to protect you."

I bent to loosen his grip, but he wouldn't let go. "Daniel, you can't come with me into the courtroom."

"Abba took me in when Saba Josiah was king. I can be quiet, Ima. I'll listen."

"Daniel, no. You—"

"Yahweh will give me wisdom." His authoritative tone startled me and captured Enoch and Hobah's attention.

I glanced up at my friends, and found Enoch smiling warmly. "Hobah and I will escort the others home. I believe Daniel needs to be with you, Atarah."

His calm assurance summoned my emotions, but I held them in check. "Thank you," I said and then licked my thumb to rub a smudge of this morning's gruel from Daniel's top lip. "And thank you, my son, for being my protector."

He offered me his hand. "Come, Ima. We should be among the royals that welcome Dohd Eliakim and his guest." Eliakim and the pharaoh reached the palace steps, and Egyptian troops stretched four soldiers wide all the way through the Kidron Valley. Terror rising, my mind whirred with new strategies to get my son out of the city.

We hurried out of the classroom and down the hall, my mind reeling. Where should we stand? Would we even be allowed entry to the court proceedings?

"Ima?" Daniel said. "Do you remember the dream I had last night?"

"Yes, love. Just a terrible nightma—" I stopped and stared down at him. "Two lion cubs, a cobra, and a beast."

He nodded. "Master Enoch told us about Jacob's son, Joseph, today. About his dreams that foretold the future. Do you think my dream told our future?"

The hairs on my arms stood straight up. "Do you remember your dream, love?" He nodded again, eyes so clear and innocent that I wanted to swim in them and wash myself clean of the world's darkness. "Remind me what your dream was about."

"The cobra bit one lion cub, and it died. But the cobra played with the other lion cub—pretending it would bite but never did. Then a big, hairy beast with giant claws came out of a gray mist and wrapped a chain around the snake and the lion cub and dragged them away." His wide eyes blinked away tears. "Do you think it means something scary, Ima?"

How could I tell my sweet boy that Judah's ensign had been the lion since their earliest days in Israel's history and Egypt's insignia a cobra. I was too frightened to imagine what army might be the beast.

"I'm not sure, love, but when Yahweh wants us to understand, I'm sure He'll tell us." I braced my son's shoulders and stared into his clear, brown eyes. "You mustn't tell anyone about the dream, Daniel. No one. Do you understand?"

He nodded again, and we resumed our hurried pace toward the throne hall. We reached the grand foyer just as Pharaoh's royal guard cleared a wide path for his arrival. King Necho was nearly a head taller than Eliakim, who followed two steps behind. Daniel and I bowed alongside other gawking spectators, but unlike the awed public, we gained entry behind other family members to King Jehoahaz's private hearing.

Instead of standing with the royals on the left, Daniel tugged me to the right, choosing a less conspicuous place among the noblemen and their families. Prince Mattaniah, his sons, the rest of Josiah's grandsons, and the royal women stood with expressions varying from terror to loathing. Had I sent Daniel home—as I'd planned—the slight could have appeared cunning, whereas standing among the noblemen gave the impression we'd already given up Daniel's claim to the throne. Whether a divinely-directed decision or merely my son's whim, I couldn't deny the wisdom of that little tug to the right.

A pall settled over the large room when Pharaoh's guards marched their king into Judah's highest court. Shallum—rather, *King Jehoahaz*—sat on his throne, his face growing paler with each step that drew King Necho and Eliakim nearer. Neither bowed when they reached the edge of the crimson carpet, barely a camel-length from the king's elevated dais.

"I welcome you to Jerusalem, mighty Pharaoh." King Jehoahaz shifted awkwardly on his throne. "Thank you for returning my brother safely. You are an honorable warrior."

Though at the right of dais, I was close enough to see pharaoh's smile and adept enough at diplomacy to know poor Shallum lost the battle before he spoke. Necho bared his brilliant white teeth, and the cobra struck Judah's lion cub.

"You, little man," Pharaoh said, pointing to King Jehoahaz,

"will no longer hide behind your mother's robe. You rule Judah no longer."

"You have no authority here." Queen Hamutal charged up the steps of the dais, and the king's royal guards surrounded her and Jehoahaz.

The king waved her off and stood. "I don't hide behind her skirts, Pharaoh Necho." He shifted his attention to Eliakim. "And, unlike my brother, I don't ask someone else to fight my battles." Eliakim grinned but remained silent.

"Then you are a coward and a fool," Necho said, still smiling. "At least your brother knows when to surrender. The new king of Judah—King Jehoiakim—will pay me one hundred talents of silver and a talent of gold each year."

The whole room gasped at such an enormous number. Now, Jehoahaz returned the pharaoh's smile. "It seems my brother has tricked you, Pharaoh Necho. Judah could never pay Assyria's tribute and you such an exorbitant amount."

Pharaoh lifted his arms, addressing everyone in the room. "Hear me, leaders of Judah. Because your former king, Josiah, slowed my attempt to aid Assyria against Babylon's western advance, the Assyrian empire has crumbled." He turned in a circle, allowing the import of the news to register. "Assyria's yoke has been broken, but now we face a new threat—Babylon's power is increasing. You can't resist them alone. Only under my protection can you stave off the new taskmaster—and it will cost your new king, Jehoiakim, one hundred talents of silver and a talent of gold per year."

He returned his attention to Jehoahaz, whose face had drained of color. "You can either surrender your throne peacefully, or I can order my troops into this courtroom and slaughter your whole family." Necho stepped back and grabbed Eliakim—the new King Jehoiakim—by the back of his neck. "Of course, to those who Judah's king shows mercy, I too extend leniency."

King Jehoahaz began to tremble. First his head, and then the tremors worked down his body and into his arms and legs. When his knees buckled, his bodyguards caught him, and Pharaoh sneered. He motioned to his Egyptian guards, who then ascended the dais and took charge of Judah's dethroned king.

"Nooo!" Hamutal beat the Egyptian guards. "Stop! How dare you—"

Necho grabbed her around the waist with one arm and held her at arm's length, too far for her short arms and legs to strike anything but air. A child's tantrum never looked so silly, but the heart of every ima in the room broke for this woman who feared the fate of her youngest son.

"What shall we do with this wildcat?" Necho asked Jehoiakim, laughing as Hamutal's hysteria settled to defeated sobs.

Before I realized he'd left my side, Daniel was climbing the steps of the dais. The whole room stilled when he tugged on Pharaoh's kilt and asked, "Is that a cobra on your head?"

Necho released Hamutal, who then hovered over my son like a protective hen. "Don't harm him," she said, lifting one arm to take a blow.

Egypt's king was no longer smiling. I rushed to the foot of the dais while he studied my son, and knelt with my head bowed low. "Please, mighty Pharaoh, I beg your forgiveness. He scampered away before I realized it. I'll—"

"Are you his mother?"

I looked up to find the Egyptian's brows drawn into a severe *v.* "Yes."

He looked to the noblemen's families. "Why didn't his father come forward? Is he a coward like—"

"You killed my father." Daniel wriggled out of Hamutal's grasp and rushed down the stairs to me. "Do you think Abba was the first lion cub in my dream, Ima?" He pointed at

Pharaoh Necho and whispered, "Judah's kings and princes wear lions on their robes, and Pharaohs wear cobras. Is the dead lion Abba, or will Pharaoh kill Dohd Shallum?"

I glanced up at Egypt's king before answering and saw both confusion and terror on his face. "This child is either a sorcerer or lunatic. What is he talking about?"

"My son had a dream last night, and he believes its fulfillment is in these events."

"Don't believe anything she says." Judah's new king hurried up the dais steps and stood beside Pharaoh Necho. "This is Johanan's wife and son. She'll say anything to put her son on the throne."

"I don't even—"

Pharaoh lifted his hand, cutting short my protest. He bent to one knee and faced Daniel. "You are a brave boy to approach a king. Now, tell me your dream. All of it. Make sure it's the truth."

Daniel recounted his dream, every detail. Pharaoh listened, nodding every so often to coax the boy along. "If Judah is the lion and Egypt the cobra, what nation is this beast you saw?" he asked when Daniel finished.

My son tapped his chin, deep in thought, and Pharaoh stifled a grin. Finally, Daniel looked him square in the eye. "I don't know, but Yahweh will show me when I need to know. Just like he showed me your cobra and Judah's lions."

"I believe he will, boy." Pharaoh stood and faced me. "Your son is a seer, lady. Both you and he will be protected."

"But mighty Pharaoh," Jehoiakim said, "you promised I could decide the fate of the royal family when you placed me on Judah's throne. You said I—"

Necho took one step toward Jehoiakim, moving the new king back. "You may rule this nation any way you wish—as long as trade routes continue to improve and I get my tribute on schedule." He swept his hand toward Daniel and me. "And as long as this woman and her gifted son are honored and protected."

Jehoiakim bowed. "I won't disappoint you mighty Pharaoh, great god of Two Lands." He straightened and glared at Hamutal. "I'll care for the rest of Judah's royal family in the ways we discussed."

EIGHT

"During Jehoiakim's reign, Nebuchadnezzar king of Babylon
invaded the land, and Jehoiakim became his vassal for three
years. But then he turned against Nebuchadnezzar and rebelled."
2 Kings 24:1

Eight Years Later

Daniel's scream launched me to my feet before I fully
woke from deep sleep. I was half-way up the roof
stairs when I realized I wore only my tunic, but my
twelve-year-old son's screams called me to the rooftop. Hananiah, Azariah, and Mishael huddled around him, trying to
shake him awake. Daniel's eyes were open, but he screamed
unintelligible cries for help.

I nudged the other boys aside and dragged my boy, who was
bigger than me, into my arms. For the third night in a row he'd
experienced this abject terror while still sleeping. *Is it the same
dream as the previous two nights, Lord? Why give him a dream
if You won't show us the meaning?*

"I'm here, love." I rocked and soothed. "Daniel, wake up.

I'm here." Slowly, his cries lessened. His hands reached around my back, and he laid his head on my shoulder. Quiet weeping told me he was awake—and remembering. "Was it the same dream?" I whispered.

"Different from the original, but the same as the last two nights."

Always so precise, my boy. "Nothing new?" *Anything, Lord. Show him something that reveals the meaning.*

"No. The beast stands on a mountain and throws a fishing net over a whole valley of very small lion cubs, taking them away in droves."

I couldn't understand why such a dream terrified him so. "Is there something you're not telling me?" A long pause sped my heartbeat, and I nudged him away to look in his eyes. "Daniel. What are you hiding?"

He looked down. "I can't tell you."

"Can't or won't?"

He shrugged off my hands and lay down on his mat. "I'm fine now, Ima. I'm sorry I woke you. Go back downstairs." The other boys returned to their mats, pulling light blankets over them on a late summer night.

Did he think a few chin hairs and his changing voice gave him the right to keep secrets from his ima? I yanked his blanket off. "You'll tell me everything right now, young man."

He scrubbed his face and let out a deep sigh. "I'm not doing it to defy you, Ima. I'm keeping you at peace by keeping silent." He sat up, kissed my cheek, and looked into my eyes. Those dark-brown eyes of his, so like his abba Johanan's. "Yahweh gives me wisdom, and I use it for our good. Trust Him if you can't trust me."

His goodness touched me so deeply, it hurt. "I wish your abba hadn't placed that burden on your shoulders, love."

"It's both burden and blessing, Ima." He kissed me again. "Go. Sleep."

With every maternal bone in my body rebelling, I returned to the chamber I shared with Enoch's and Hobah's maid. She was snoring, evidently not too disturbed by Daniel's outburst. Sleep refused to come, and I watched darkness turn to day. All the usual busyness of our over-stuffed household marched on, ignoring the huge hole in my heart where my husband used to be and that my growing son made wider. Enoch prepared his shoulder bag to leave for class while the four boys—Daniel, Hananiah, Mishael, and Azariah—finished up their morning gruel. At the beginning of the new year, the two older boys would turn thirteen and begin their military training in Judah's ranks. The thought terrified me almost as much as Daniel's secrets.

"May I have another bowl of gruel?" Mishael asked.

Hobah looked as if she might burst into tears. "I'm sorry, son, but—"

"You can have mine," I said, pushing my bowl toward the round-faced twin. "I'm not very hungry this morning."

His ima started to protest, but I lifted a brow in silent warning. We'd rationed the grain to the kernel for this week's meals. Everyone in Judah made sacrifices when King Jehoiakim raised taxes to meet Pharaoh Necho's exorbitant tribute demands. Staples like wheat, barley, and wine—usually plentiful in Jerusalem—had become sparse even for noblemen in the Upper City. Thankfully, my royal allowance and Daniel's were steady, only because early in Jehoiakim's reign, Necho's spies had reported one of Judah's royal guards harassing me. The guard's right arm was delivered to Jehoiakim a week later, along with a scroll explaining it would be Jehoiakim's arm the next time Daniel or I suffered offense. My monthly allowance had never been late, and no one bothered us at Enoch's home.

"Thank you, Mistress Atarah." Mishael hovered over his bowl as if any one of the boys might steal it. His twin, Azariah, was the only one mischievous enough to taunt him.

My stomach rumbled, betraying my hunger, so I shot to my feet and grabbed a large jug. "I'll get today's water, Hobah."

"No!" Daniel was on his feet, blocking the door before I'd taken my second step. A room full of silent stares begged the question.

"Is there something you'd like to tell me about Jerusalem's water supply?" I asked my wide-eyed son.

He was suddenly too interested in his sandals, so I looked to the other boys and found them equally fascinated with anything but their parents' inquiring stares.

Fists on my hips, I turned to the other adults in the room. "I'll take Daniel to the courtyard. Hobah, you take Hananiah to your chamber. And Enoch questions the twins where they sit. We'll get to the truth."

Hobah gripped Hananiah's arm like a vice and was halfway to her chamber when Daniel let out a defeated sigh. "At the first sign of a siege, the city cistern will be unsafe for any one of us. We'll need to go in pairs."

I shot a panicked glance at Enoch. "Is Jerusalem coming under siege?"

He shook his head and called Hobah and Hananiah back to the leather mat we used as a table. "Daniel, are you worried about a siege because we've been studying the battle King Josiah and your abba fought in? The Babylonians defeated the Assyrians in that battle and have gained strength over the years, but—"

"They gained enough strength that Judah paid tribute to *both* Babylon and Egypt for three years."

"Yes." Enoch held his gaze.

"But Dohd Jehoiakim stopped paying tribute six months ago—to both of them."

Enoch shot a concerned glance at me, and it was my turn to be perplexed. He asked Daniel, "How do you know Jehoiakim stopped paying tribute?"

But if Enoch didn't know, I didn't want Daniel to tell palace business and put our friends at risk. "Come outside with me," I said, setting aside the water jug and leading my son to the courtyard for a more private conversation.

He answered the question on my mind before we reached the shade of the myrtle tree. "No one told me Dohd Jehoiakim stopped paying tribute," he said. "I just know because, in my new dream, the beast watches from a mountainside while a large male lion eats and drinks his fill. The lion beats and mistreats his cubs, caging and starving them. When the beast sees the cubs are almost dead, he slays the lion, unlocks the cage, and throws a fishnet over some of the cubs. Then the cubs are carried away by a giant hand in the sky, and the beast returns to burn and destroy every green tree and living creature where the lion cubs once frolicked and played." Tears ran in rivulets down my son's cheeks as he seemed to see the dream lived out in the retelling.

I reached up to wipe away a tear, but he brushed my hand aside. "Ima, Babylon is the beast, and they're coming. Dohd Jehoiakim will let all of Judah starve while the beast marches into our towns and cities, destroying everything Yahweh promised to His chosen people."

Staring at my heart-broken son, I hoped Yahweh had shown him only the broad strokes of Jehoiakim's abominable sins. He'd taken every woman in the palace to his bed to prove supremacy over his family. Those who refused, he killed, along with dozens of his own soldiers so he could seize their wives and their land. He worshiped every pagan god and tattooed their images all over his body.

"Jehoiakim is no lion," I said. "He's lower than a snake and will someday receive his due punishment."

"He is a king in the lineage of King David, Ima, but even he isn't safe from Yahweh's judgment. None of us are."

His calm certainty was terrifying, and then I remembered the rest of the dream. "What does the fishnet mean, Daniel?"

He pulled me into his arms. "It means I'll be taken from you, Ima." The words felt like a spear piercing my chest. He held me tighter. "But please don't worry. I believe we'll both live under Yahweh's protection."

I lingered in my son's embrace, remembering the day I said goodbye to Johanan. That day I memorized everything about him. His smell had faded from my memory, his voice now silent in my mind. But our son, now equal to me in height, had surely surpassed both his parents in understanding. "Your abba would be proud of you, Daniel."

I felt his whole body shake with sobs and knew that my boy missed his abba more than he ever confessed. Holding him, I let the tears cleanse him and the sniffing clear his voice. He rubbed my back and made no effort to escape my arms. "He was more than my abba. He was my hero."

Smiling through tears, I whispered, "Mine too, but *you*, Daniel ben Johanan, are my champion."

Author's Note

Clear as mud?

There is much debate among scholars about the reigns of Judah's kings and the details of Babylon's rise to power. The historical identity of Amyitis is also hotly contested. Was she a sister to King Astyages or his daughter? Was Mandane—the mother of Cyrus the Great—Amyitis's sister (as in the story)? Or was Amyitis actually Cyrus's wife? This is an important question since years later Cyrus grows up to conquer both the Medes and Babylonians!

I chose to make Amyitis Nebuchadnezzar's bride because of the legend that says Babylon's famous Hanging Gardens—one of the seven wonders of the ancient world—were actually built by Nebuchadnezzar as a gift for Queen Amyitis. In the dry and dusty desert of Babylon, his wife missed her homeland—the Zagros Mountains—so the ruthless king showed his romantic side by building the lavish gardens to ease her homesickness.

Equally confusing are Josiah's sons whose names were changed when they became Judah's kings. Eliakim was later renamed Jehoiakim by Pharaoh Neco (2 Kings 23:34). Mattaniah was later renamed Zedekiah by Nebuchadnezzar (2 Kings 24:17). And Shallum was also called Jehoahaz (Jeremiah 22:11).

Military Genius

When the Babylonians and Medes banded together with other tribes and nations against the Assyrians, they successfully conquered Nineveh and broke the chokehold of a centuries-old empire known for its insane cruelty. But part of Assyria's defeat must also be attributed to the delay of one of their strongest allies—Egypt.

For an unknown reason, Egypt's Pharaoh Necho had agreed to help Assyria fight Babylon's aggression. In an equally confusing decision, Judah's King Josiah marched his troops out to fight against Necho in the northern Israel city of Megiddo. Many believe it was King Josiah's delay of Egypt's troops that won the battle for Babylon and ultimately destroyed Assyria's long and powerful world rule. King Josiah, like us, had no idea how his single decision would affect the world, his kingdom, his family, or the little boy named...Daniel.

His mother, Atarah, is a completely fictionalized character whose name means, *crown*. I chose King Josiah's firstborn, Johanan, as Daniel's father because he's mentioned only in 1 Chronicles 3:15 and never again. As the king's firstborn, he would have likely taken the throne if he had lived through the battle at Megiddo. We don't know if Daniel was descended from King David's royal line or a nobleman's son, but he would have been one or the other.

> "In the third year of the reign of Jehoiakim king of Judah, Nebuchadnezzar king of Babylon came to Jerusalem and besieged it. And the Lord delivered Jehoiakim king of Judah into his hand . . . Then the king ordered Ashpenaz, chief of his court officials, to bring into the king's service some of the Israelites from

the royal family and the nobility." *Daniel 1:1-3*

Research uncovered a few glitches in the timeline and reigns of Jehoahaz/Shallum and Jehoiakim/Eliakim. For instance, 2 Kings 23:33 says King Necho put bronze shackles on Jehoahaz in Riblah, but 2 Chronicles 36:3 says Pharaoh dethroned him in Jerusalem. Since we know Scripture never lies, we can imagine that Jehoahaz may have been stripped of his royal title in Jerusalem and later shackled as a prisoner in Riblah.

2 Chronicles 36:5 tells us Jehoiakim reigned for eleven years. 2 Kings 24:1-4 says Nebuchadnezzar invaded and made Jehoiakim his vassal for three years and thereafter rebelled. Did Nebuchadnezzar replace him in that third year? No one seems to know. Some believe his own soldiers threw him over the walls —he was THAT despised. Regardless of how he died, his son, *Jehoiachin*, succeeded him on the throne and ruled a whopping three months.

Nebuchadnezzar ended the siege, broke through Jerusalem's walls, and placed Jehoiachin's uncle on the throne —a third son of Josiah named, Mattaniah. Since Nebuchadnezzar was all about confusion, he changed Mattaniah's name to *Zedekiah*. He was the last king of Judah, led away to Babylon when Nebuchadnezzar completely destroyed Jerusalem in 586 B.C..

I hope the prequel of *Heroes and Kings* helped clarify both Nebuchadnezzar's and Daniel's early lives and will make *Of Fire and Lions* even more powerful because you'll understand some of the history leading up to Judah's exile. If you'd like to know more about the destruction of Jerusalem in particular, please check out my novella, *By the Waters of Babylon,* based on Psalm 137, the Captive's Psalm.

About the Author

MESU ANDREWS is the Christy Award-winning author of *Isaiah's Daughter* whose deep understanding of and love for God's Word brings the biblical world alive for readers. Mesu lives in North Carolina with her husband Roy. She stays connected with readers through newsie emails, fun blog posts, and frequent short stories. For more information, visit Mesu-Andrews.com.

Also by Mesu Andrews

Love Amid the Ashes

Love's Sacred Song

Love in a Broken Vessel

In the Shadow of Jezebel

The Pharaoh's Daughter

Miriam

Isaiah's Daughter

By the Waters of Babylon

Of Fire and Lions

Isaiah's Legacy

The Reluctant Rival: Leah's Story

Potiphar's Wife

In Feast or Famine

Made in the USA
Monee, IL
18 November 2022

18063992R00129